WAR PARTY

Wayne D. Overholser

Chivers Press • G.K. Hall & Co.
Bath, England • Thorndike, Maine USA

This Large Print edition is published by Chivers Press, England, and by G.K. Hall & Co., USA.

Published in 1997 in the U.K. by arrangement with Golden West Literary Agency.

Published in 1997 in the U.S. by arrangement with Golden West Literary Agency.

U.K. Hardcover   ISBN 0–7451–8857–5 (Chivers Large Print)
U.K. Softcover   ISBN 0–7451–8883–4 (Camden Large Print)
U.S. Softcover   ISBN 0–7838–2004–6 (Nightingale Collection Edition)

The text of this Large Print edition is unabridged.
Other aspects of the book may vary from the original edition.

Set in 16 pt. New Times Roman.

Printed in Great Britain on acid-free paper.

British Library Cataloguing in Publication Data available

Library of Congress Cataloging-in-Publication Data

Daniels, John S., 1906–
    War party : John S. Daniels.
        p.   cm.
    ISBN 0–7838–2004–6 (lg. print : sc)
    1. Large type books.   I. Title.
[PS3529.V33W3   1997]
813′.54—dc20   96–44968

CHAPTER ONE

Ben Holt pitched the last forkful of hay onto the wagon as he glanced at the dark clouds hanging over the Continental Divide to the east. He had beaten the rain and saved every shock of hay. Now he could button up for the winter. The way it felt on this morning of September 30, 1879, winter wasn't far away. The bite of fall had been in the air for days.

He tossed his pitchfork onto the load of hay and started to climb aboard, then froze, his right foot on the hub of the front wheel. Someone was riding upstream toward him on the dead run. The horseman was too far down the Yampa river for Ben to see him clearly, but from the cloud of dust that was being raised, he judged the rider was coming fast. Something was wrong, he told himself, dead wrong, to make a man ride like that.

Ben climbed to the top of the load and, picking up the lines, put his team into a gallop. The wagon with its bulky load lurched over the rough ground, then reached the road that ran along the east bank of the river. The dust rose behind him in a gray fog that drifted slowly away as the damp breeze from the high peaks caught it.

A prickle of uneasiness ran down Ben's spine as he wondered if the Utes had finally gone on

1

the warpath. The reservation line was only a few miles to the west, and ever since the time he had staked his claim, every settler on the Yampa knew that he was flirting with death, that he was taking a calculated gamble with the odds against him.

The White River Utes were notorious for drifting off the reservation when they were on their hunting forays, and they made no secret of their hatred for Nathan Meeker, their agent. Several had even made the long trip to Denver to lay their complaints before Governor Pitkin, but Meeker had not been removed.

Still, the Utes had never been famous as fighters in the sense the Sioux, Apaches and Comanches had been. Almost everyone on the Yampa, from Hank Long who had a trading post far down the river to Maudie Kregg who owned the next farm south of Ben's place, said the Utes wouldn't actually do anything, that their meanness didn't go past the talking point.

Glancing back, Ben saw that the rider had cut the distance between them in half. Usually Ben took his Winchester with him when he left the house, but he hadn't today. Now he wished he had it. If the horseman was being chased by a band of Utes, and if they overtook Ben before he reached his house, he was a goner.

He breathed easier when he swung off the road toward his barn. Apparently no one was behind the rider. At least there was no other dust as far as he could see back to where the hills closed in on both sides of the river.

Ben slid to the ground the instant the team stopped beside the corral; he sprinted to the house and grabbed his Winchester from the antler rack just inside the door. As he wheeled and ran back to the wagon he was sick with the thought that if an Indian war had broken out the Utes would probably raid across the reservation line and burn the buildings of every ranch on the river.

Ben had settled on the Yampa two years before; he had put up his buildings and cleared a hay field and cleared the willows from the river bank directly in front of the house. He had built well, hauling pine logs for his house and barn from the mountains instead of using the cottonwoods that grew along the stream.

He leaned his rifle against the corral, unhooked the team and led the horses into the barn, then stripped harness from them and hung it on pegs driven into the logs of the wall. All the time the thought kept nagging him that his hard work would be wasted if he walked off and left his place undefended. He couldn't do it. He wouldn't do it. By the time he stepped outside, he had made his decision. He would stay here.

The rider had reined off the road and now pulled up beside the wagon. Ben recognized him, Carl Niven who had a ranch between the settlement of Hayden and Long's trading post.

'Run for your life,' Niven yelled as he swung

out of the saddle. 'The Utes have murdered Meeker and everybody else on the agency. They ambushed Major Thornburgh who was taking a column of soldiers onto the reservation. Thornburgh and a lot of his men are dead. The rest are pinned down on Milk Creek and the damned Injuns have got 'em surrounded and are pouring lead at 'em as fast as they can pull the triggers.'

Ben stared at the rancher, unable to believe this. The situation was worse than he had imagined in his wildest fears. He saw that Niven was dead-tired. So was his horse. It had been a long ride from the man's ranch so he had reason to be tired. But what he had just said was so incredible that Ben couldn't accept it. Sure, the Utes hated Meeker enough to kill him and Ben could believe that, but to pin down a column of soldiers and kill their commanding officer was too much.

Ben fell into step with Niven as the rancher led his sweat-gummed horse to the trough and watered him. Ben asked, 'How'd you hear this, Carl?'

Niven turned on him angrily. 'You think I made this up? You think I'd kill myself and my horse to warn you and your neighbors if...'

'No,' Ben cut in, 'and I thank you for bringing the word, but I know how stories like this grow. I just asked how you heard it.'

Niven pointed to a red welt along his right cheek. 'They took some shots at me two, three miles from here. I got this.' He took off his hat and rammed a thumb through a bullet hole in the crown. 'And this.' He put his hat back on and glared at Ben. 'You think maybe that was part of the story somebody told me?'

'No,' Ben admitted, 'but I'd still like to know how you heard about what had happened.'

Dust had settled in the week-old stubble on Niven's face, giving it the pallor of a dead man. He washed, then bent down to drink from the pipe that brought water to the trough from a spring behind the house. He straightened and wiped his mouth with the back of his hand.

'Joe Rankin was guiding Thornburgh, but he sure as hell didn't keep the soldiers from walking into a trap. If it had been me, or old Jim Baker...'

Niven stopped and shook his head. 'No sense faulting anybody now. What's done is done and it can't be undone. Anyhow, Rankin and John Gordon and a couple of soldiers got through the Ute lines last night. I talked to 'em. That's how I heard. Rankin's going on to Rawlins to get help and Gordon's warning the settlers. I told him I'd cut across Twenty Mile Park and tell you folks on the upper river. Now are you gonna saddle up and ride out of here with me?'

Ben shook his head. 'I'm staying. If the Utes want my hair, they're gonna have to work for it.'

'Have you gone daft, man?' Niven

5

demanded. 'You can't hold off a band of Injuns by yourself. Some of the settlers are holing up in Steamboat Springs and some in Hayden, so they'll be safe enough, but the best thing for you and your neighbors to do is to hike out for Middle Park. Once you get over Gore Pass...'

'I've got just two neighbors,' Ben interrupted. 'Justin Miles and his daughter Cherry live across the river, and Maudie Kregg and her grandson Bucky have got a place upstream about a mile. You warn Maudie when you go by her house and I'll see that Justin Miles gets word.'

Niven shot a glance downstream the way he had come as if expecting a band of Indians to break into the open any second, then he swung back to face Ben. 'Holt, you've been eating loco weed. Get out of here while you've still got your hair. I tell you that once you get across Gore Pass into Middle Park, you'll be safe.'

Ben saw that fear possessed Carl Niven; the kind of belly-deep fear that made a man do and say things he would not have said or done under normal circumstances. But he had every right to be scared, Ben told himself. Niven had talked to Joe Rankin and John Gordon about what had happened on Milk Creek, and he'd been shot at by the Indians and could easily have been killed.

Still, ambushing a column of soldiers that had crossed the reservation boundary was one

6

thing, but attacking settlers who had not harmed the Indians and burning ranches that were outside the reservation was something else.

Ben shook his head. 'Thanks for warning me, Carl. I'll keep my eyes open, but I'm not pulling out for Middle Park. I've got a solid log house that won't burn easy, especially if it rains which it looks like it's going to. I'll try to get Justin Miles and his girl to move in with me. You tell Maudie that the boy and her are welcome too. I've got a hunch she'd rather stay here than run to Middle Park.'

'Oh hell,' Niven said in disgust. 'It's your business if you want to lose your hair, but there ain't nothing here worth dying for.'

'Depends on the way you look at it,' Ben said. 'It was my sweat and blood that went into making this ranch, Carl. It wasn't yours. I knew the chance I was taking when I came. Give me another ten years and, with a little luck, I'll be a rich man; but if I go off and leave it and they burn me out, I'd have to start over. I can't do it.'

Ben looked at the peeled logs that made up the walls of his cabin. They had been carefully notched at the corners, the doors and windows were fitted tightly, and he had spent hours chinking the sides with clay so that even on windy days he did not feel the slightest draft inside the house.

He shook his head, thinking of the years he

7

had drifted from one job to another, as rootless as a tumbleweed, and how by sheer accident he had wandered over Gore Pass. He remembered the first time he had looked at this spot and had told himself immediately it was going to be his home.

He glanced at Niven and shook his head again. 'No, I can't do it. Call me daft or say I've been eating loco weed, but I can't leave here. Now that I know what's happened, I won't be surprised.'

'The hell you won't,' Niven snapped. 'I know them red bastards better'n you do. I've watched 'em come into Long's trading post. Jack. Colorow. Sowerwick. A lot more of 'em. I've heard 'em talk about Meeker and what they'd do if he ever sent for the soldiers. He told 'em that if they didn't behave, he'd put 'em in chains and send 'em to Indian Territory or Florida. Jack speaks purty good English. He knew what Meeker was talking about, and he said right out that he'd rather die here fighting for his home than be sent away in chains.'

'I don't blame him,' Ben said. 'I'd feel the same way if I was a Ute.'

'You're soft.' Niven's lips drew away from his brown teeth as he glared at Ben. 'I hope Rankin brings back a thousand soldiers and they kill every Ute they find.'

'They'd better start with Hank Long,' Ben said sharply. 'If he hadn't traded with the Utes, give 'em guns and ammunition after Meeker

8

told him not to, this wouldn't have happened.'

Niven glanced back up the valley again, turned to look at the fringe of timber on the hills across the river, then swung into his saddle. 'I ain't augerin' about Hank Long,' Niven said. 'If some of the settlers don't stretch his neck afore this is over, I'll be surprised.'

'How did Rankin and Gordon know Meeker's been murdered?' Ben asked. 'The soldiers never got to the agency if they're pinned down on Milk Creek.'

'Rankin didn't see the bodies,' Niven admitted, 'but Meeker's the man the Injuns hate. You think they'd let him live after they stopped the soldiers the way they done? Of course they've killed him. Slow and mean, too. You can bet on it. There's three women and two little kids at the agency. Think what's happened to them afore you waste any sympathy on the red devils. They're your friends one minute, then they turn on you and they're animals.'

Niven whirled his horse and rode away. Shrugging, Ben stepped into the corral and caught and saddled his black gelding. He told himself he'd been stupid to raise the question about Meeker's death. He knew as well as Niven did how much the Utes hated the agent.

More than once Jack and Sowerwick and other chiefs had stopped and he had fed them. They considered him their friend as certainly as they considered Justin Miles their enemy.

9

Miles had refused to feed them and had even driven them away from his cabin with his shotgun. He had ridiculed Ben for being friendly with the Utes and had called him 'soft,' the same adjective Niven had applied to him a minute or two ago.

Suddenly angry, Ben jammed his Winchester into the boot and stepped into the saddle. He wasn't soft. He was smart. That was all. As he rode toward the river, the anger suddenly left him. Being smart or soft had nothing to do with the way he had treated the Indians.

The truth was he had felt sympathy for the Indians the same as he would have felt sympathy for wild animals that had been penned up. Nathan Meeker had tried to domesticate them overnight, an error in judgment that had undoubtedly cost him his life.

Fording the river, Ben turned upstream toward Justin Miles's cabin. He guessed he understood the Utes better than most whites because his youthful, rootless years had been about as wild as they could be, short of actually taking him outside the law. If anyone had tried to tame him by force during those years he would have become a killer just as the Utes had.

As he thought back over his twenty-seven years, he wasn't sure what had changed him except that he had finally seen the futility of his way of life. Too, something strange and wonderful had happened when he had looked at this spot on the Yampa. He had never been here before; obviously then, he had never seen it, but it had seemed to be familiar; he had had the feeling he had come home at last.

For a time Ben had been the only settler on this stretch of the river, then Maudie Kregg and her grandson Bucky had come. At first he resented having neighbors, but his attitude changed. He liked Maudie and he soon became fond of Bucky. Later, after Justin Miles and Cherry had moved in across the river, he'd fallen in love with Cherry, although she seemed indifferent to him.

He put his horse into a gallop, a sense of urgency suddenly taking possession of him. After what had happened on Milk Creek any friendship he'd had with Jack and Sowerwick and the other chiefs would be forgotten. He guessed he didn't care much what happened to Justin Miles who was as lazy and ornery an old goat as he'd ever run into, but he cared a lot about what happened to Cherry.

CHAPTER TWO

Ben heard angry voices from inside the Miles cabin when he dismounted. Cherry and her father were at it again, he thought. He often

11

wondered why the girl had stayed with Justin Miles as long as she had.

Miles was a good fisherman and hunter, but that was about all Ben could say for him. He was fifty-two years old, he was in the best of health, and he was big enough and strong enough to have carved a good farm out of the wilderness on the west bank of the Yampa, but work was the last thing he wanted to do.

Miles had cleared the sagebrush off a field that was about as big as a postage stamp. He raised barely enough hay to get his team through the winter if they had a late fall and an early spring, but now with September almost gone the hay was still in the shock. He hadn't finished the pole fence around the pasture; he hadn't even hauled enough wood to last until Christmas.

Ben hesitated, hearing Miles say defensively, 'I had to fish hard to catch 'em. They wasn't biting good, but I finally got 'em. They're big enough to give us a good meal. The smallest one's a foot long.'

'You and your silly pride about catching three fish,' Cherry cried. 'Well, let me tell you something. If you don't cut enough wood to cook them, you won't have any fish for dinner. And when are you going to haul the rest of the wood down from the hill? Or are you going to leave it where it is until we get two feet of snow on the ground? You've got hay to haul and a fence to finish, and you keep saying you're going to chink . . .'

'All right, all right. I'll cut the wood while you clean the trout.' He stopped and took a long breath, then he burst out, 'I put meat on the table, don't I? You never have starved and you never will as long as you keep house for me.'

Ben moved to the front door of the cabin, but Cherry and her father were so engrossed in their quarrel that neither noticed him. Cherry said passionately, 'Maybe I won't starve, but I don't have a decent dress to my name and no money to buy cloth to make one. I'll freeze again this winter just like I did last year because of the shoddy job you did when you built the cabin. I'll have to listen to you complain about wading in snow up to your crotch to get wood you should have hauled before now. I'll be boiling deer bones for soup . . .'

Ben cleared his throat. Cherry and her father whirled to face him, Cherry's face turning red and Miles opening his mouth and shutting it without saying a word. He was a man who hid behind a facade of dignity, but now it was stripped from him and for the moment he was too embarrassed to say a word.

'The Utes have gone crazy,' Ben said. 'They're on the war path and it's not safe for you folks to stay here. I want you to stay with me till the trouble's over. We can do a purty good job defending ourselves if we get together, but if we stay in our own cabins,

13

they'll get all of us.'

Miles acted as if he didn't hear what Ben said. He bellowed, 'You've sure got your gall, Holt, sneaking up on us without letting us know you're within a mile of our place.'

'It wasn't Ben's fault, Pa,' Cherry said. 'We were yelling at each other so loud you wouldn't have heard it thunder.'

'And you wouldn't have heard any Indians if they'd come calling,' Ben said. 'Now pick up whatever you'll need for a few days and come to my place. Chances are we don't have much time.'

'Go to your place, you say,' Miles said, still angry. 'Well, sir, I've got a better idea, Holt. Go back to your house and pick up what you need and come here. We can defend ourselves in my cabin as easy as we can in yours.'

'No, Pa,' Cherry said. 'We'll go to Ben's place.'

'Why?' Miles demanded hotly. 'I don't see no reason to go off and leave my cabin empty so they can burn it. Let 'em burn his.'

'Ben built a solid cabin that can be defended,' Cherry said. 'Ours can't.' She pointed to a crack between two logs. 'If they attack us here, bullets would be flying all over the place. They wouldn't in Ben's cabin.'

Miles glared at his daughter, then stomped outside, pushing Ben out of his way. He called back, 'I'll go cut that wood you ordered.'

Cherry remained where she stood in the

14

middle of the cabin. She said, embarrassed, 'I'm sorry you caught us quarreling, but I guess you're not surprised. All of a sudden I just got to the end of my rope. Pa is the most shiftless man on the Yampa. I can't stand living from hand to mouth the way I have all my life. Not any more.'

She motioned toward the wall to her right. 'Look at it, Ben. You can see daylight between half of the logs and around the door and all the windows. My lean-to room is pretty tight, but I can't stay in it all the time. Tomorrow is the first of October. We may get a snow any day now, and we're not prepared for it any better than we were a year ago.'

She stopped and stared at him as if only then realizing what she was saying and who she was talking to. A hand came up to her throat. She said, her voice low, 'I'm sorry, Ben. I didn't aim to blow off like that.'

She dropped into a chair, too ashamed to look at him. She was twenty-one, Ben knew, a strong, robust girl who had attracted him from the first time he had seen her. She had auburn hair, blue eyes, and good features, but more important to him was her pleasant disposition.

He had never seen her angry before; he had never heard her talk to anyone in the tone she had just used on her father. Now, looking at her, he wondered which was the real Cherry, the pleasant girl he had known, or the furious harridan he had surprised a few minutes before.

He was shocked by the scene he had stumbled onto so that, for the moment, he had forgotten why he had come. Remembering, he said, 'I don't know how much time we've got, but I know we've wasted too much already. It's Justin's business if he wants to stay here and get murdered, but you've got to come with me. Of course you and Justin can hitch up your wagon and light out for Middle Park, but I think you'll be safer in my place.'

She looked up, tears running down her cheeks. She said, 'Ben, please don't think I scream at other people the way I was at Pa when you came in. I've nagged him so much about the work he ought to do and won't. It doesn't do any good. I guess I went out of my head.'

'Cherry, please get whatever you need for the next few days,' Ben said. 'You can ride behind me. We've taken too much time, I tell you. If you're worried about being alone with me, I think Maudie Kregg and Bucky will be along.'

She rose. 'I'll get my things. I'm not afraid of being alone with you. Don't think that.'

She disappeared into the lean-to room. Ben stepped outside, hearing the steady chunk-chunk of Miles's ax, but he didn't say anything to the man until Cherry appeared carrying a carpet bag.

'Justin,' Ben called.

16

Miles stopped work, laid the ax down, and turned slowly. He said in a surly voice, 'Well?'

'You can't stay here,' Ben said. 'If you don't want to live with me for a few days, hitch up your wagon and light out for Gore Pass. You'll probably be safe once you get to Middle Park.'

'How'd you hear about all this Injun trouble?' Miles demanded.

Ben told him briefly, and added, 'I don't figure the scare will last more'n a few days. A relief party from Fort Steele will show up and the Utes will scatter. You can stand me and Maudie Kregg and Bucky for that long, so you'd better change your mind and move in with us.'

Miles's thick-lipped mouth turned down at the corners as if he had just tasted something bitter. He said, 'Holt, you're mighty damned smart the way you moved into the valley and worked your tail off and built that fine place o' your'n. You've given my girl something to point at while she cusses me for not working. Well sir, I wouldn't be beholden to you for nothing, not even my life. Cherry, if you leave here and move in with Holt, don't ever come back."

'I don't intend to, Pa,' she said. 'There must be a better way to live than this.'

Turning, she walked to Ben's horse and stood there until he came. He mounted and she swung up behind him, her right arm holding to him, her carpetbag in her left hand. Her skirt

17

was pulled high on her trim legs, but it was the only way she could ride. She didn't show the slightest trace of embarrassment, or that she was even aware of the way she looked to Ben.

'Hang on,' Ben said. 'We're going to get across the river without wasting any more time.'

He glanced again at the fringe of quaking aspens on the hills to the west, thinking that if a raiding party of Utes suddenly erupted from the trees, he'd never make it to his cabin with Cherry.

He felt her right arm tighten around him as he dug in the spurs, felt the side of her face pressed against his back. He didn't slow up when they reached the river. The cold, clear water sprayed out on both sides of them as the black's hoofs struck the surface, looking like silver spangles in the morning light. Then they were across and he was reining up in front of his house.

'We made it,' he said as she slid to the ground. 'No way to know whether we're scared over nothing or not, but it would be crazy to take any chances finding out.'

'I guess Pa will find out,' she said. 'He's just stubborn and ornery enough to act clean crazy.'

'Go on in and make yourself at home,' he said, 'I'll be back in a minute.'

He rode on to the corral, thinking she was exactly right about Justin Miles.

CHAPTER THREE

Ben stripped the gear from his horse, turned him into the corral and, snatching up his rifle from where he had leaned it against the corral fence, hurried back to the house. He found Cherry standing in the center of his living room looking at the furniture and the board floor and the stone fireplace.

She smiled when he came in. 'Ben, I can't believe it. You settled here just a little while before we did, and you've done all this. It's a fine, tight house, better even than I thought it was. Why, it would be good enough for a town house.'

'Oh, I don't know about that.' He was pleased by what she had said, and he let her see the pride that he felt in his work. 'A lot of sweat went into the house. The barn, too. It took most of last winter during the bad weather to make the furniture.'

He hung his Winchester on the antler rack by the door and turned to her. 'It's the reason I wouldn't run when Carl Niven stopped and told me about the Indians. If they come by and find the place empty they'll burn it, but maybe if we throw a little lead in their direction, they'll ride on by.'

'I can help fight,' she said. 'I'm a pretty good shot.'

19

'I know you are, but this can be purty risky. If you haven't thought about that you'd better start thinking. Maybe Maudie and the boy will move in with us and we can divide things up so some of us can sleep. We'll have four guns if we're attacked. What you ought to think about is that there may be just the two of us.'

'I'm not afraid,' she said simply. 'I don't think I'd be afraid of anything if you were with me.'

Ben gave her a searching look. She had never said anything like that to him before. He guessed he just didn't understand her. He had known for a long time that she did not get along with her father. That was no puzzle, Justin Miles being the kind of man he was, but Ben didn't know how she felt about him. She had always been courteous when he'd called on her, even appearing to welcome his visits, but when he touched her, either by accident or intent, she drew back as if the slightest contact with any part of his body was distasteful to her.

'I've a quarter of venison hanging from a pole outside,' he said. 'I'll slice off a couple of steaks and start a fire if you want to get dinner.'

'Of course I do.' She was still looking around the room as if comparing it to the dirt-floored cabin her father had built. 'You did all of this yourself, didn't you?'

'All but the fireplace,' he said. 'There's a man in Steamboat Springs who's good at making fireplaces, so I hauled the rocks and hired him to build it.' He motioned to the doors in the back wall. 'The one on the right goes into the kitchen. The other one leads into the bedroom. You'll have to change the bedding. There's some clean blankets on the shelves over the foot of the bed. If Maudie comes, you'll have to share the bed with her.'

She grimaced. 'It'll be the same as sleeping with a fat sow. If she rolls over on me, I'll be squashed like a little pig.'

Ben grinned. 'Oh, I guess she's not that heavy.'

'Where will you sleep?'

He nodded at the couch. 'I built that for sleeping if I ever had company which I've never had before. There's a wool tick under the blankets. Many's the time I've stretched out on it after supper and gone to sleep with a big fire in the fireplace.'

'Let me sleep out here, Ben. I don't want to run you out of your bed.'

'No.' He said it more sharply than he intended, and added quickly, 'I didn't aim to snarl at you, but the bedroom is yours. I wouldn't have it any other way. Even with me sleeping out here, this is going to ruin your reputation if Maudie don't come, but maybe folks won't hear about it.'

'I'm not going to worry about it, Ben,' she said briskly. 'Now if you'll get a fire started, I'll rustle up something for dinner.'

'Cherry.' He moved toward her, then

21

stopped a step away. He wasn't sure this was the time to tell her how he felt, but maybe there would never be a better time. 'I want to say something first. I'm proud of what I've done with this place the two years I've been here, though I'm sure not proud of the years before I got here. I wasted them just drifting around.'

He walked to the door and stood motionless, looking at the willows and cottonwoods that lined the banks of the river, except at the ford where he had cleared a space fifty feet wide. He stared absently at the timbered ridge beyond the river, the aspens making gold streaks through the spruce. He had intended to say he loved her and to ask her to marry him, but somehow he'd started off wrong.

He swung around to face her. 'I'm not sure what changed me, Cherry, except that I saw what could be done here. No one else lived in this part of the valley when I came, so I had my pick of places to settle. I began thinking about what the future could mean, and well, it seemed like a challenge I couldn't turn down.

'Cherry, what I'm trying to say is that I stayed and I worked and I've got a good place started. I'm not rich, but I've got a few cows and calves, a good saddle horse and a purty fair team. What I don't have is money, but in another year or two I'll have some steers to sell. The way it is now, a man can live off the country.'

His mouth was dry. The right words just

22

didn't seem to come. He studied the timber across the river again, then the brush along the stream, searching for anything that would indicate the presence of Indians, but there was nothing.

All the time he was trying to think of just the right way to say what he wanted to say, but the pretty and romantic words that a woman liked to hear didn't come to him, so he blurted, 'I love you, Cherry. I want to marry you. Will you have me?'

'Ben, Ben,' she whispered. 'I want to marry you. I want to marry you more than anything else in the world, but I can't. Not the way things are now.'

'Why? You're not married, are you?'

'No,' she answered quickly. 'It's Pa. Sometimes I hate him, but I love him, too. He needs me. I can't leave him and I couldn't marry you and ask you to support him.'

'He told you not to come back.'

'He didn't mean it,' she said. 'He'll be glad to see me when this is over.'

Ben shook his head grimly. 'I'll bet he will. What he wants is a housekeeper, but it ain't right any way you look at it. I love you, Cherry. I can't give you a palace to live in ...'

'Don't say that, Ben,' she said sternly. 'Can't you understand? It wouldn't make any difference to me if you didn't have a horse or a cow or even this house. It's just that I will not let Pa be a burden to you.'

Suddenly he was irritated. She was being crazy stubborn and not making any sense. She couldn't meet his gaze. She was trembling, then he saw the shiny beads of moisture that had gathered on her forehead, and the irritation was gone.

He thought he understood. Her father was a weakling. He didn't deserve her, but he was her father. She was right in saying that Justin Miles needed her. Still, it was wrong for her to stay single because she had a shiftless father who needed her.

For a moment he hesitated, thinking there was only one thing to do. If that didn't work, he'd give up. He took her into his arms and, placing a hand under her chin, tipped her head back. She was crying, and suddenly, knowing how her life had been with Justin Miles, he felt a great sympathy for her.

'We'll figure something out for Justin,' he said.

He pulled her to him and kissed her long and hard. At first she did not respond. Her body was rigid, her lips were pressed tightly together, then her control broke, and she became a living flame in his arms.

She hugged him with all of her strength, her body pressed against his; her lips were soft and sweet, her surrender so complete that he could not doubt her love for him. She understood what tenderness was, perhaps for the first time in her life.

She drew back finally, a small smile touching the corners of her mouth. 'Ben,' she asked unsteadily, 'do you know what you've done to me?'

'I think I do,' he said, 'and I sure know what you did to me. Now will you marry me?'

'I want to, Ben,' she said. 'I want to very...'

A volley of shots and Indian yells broke into her words. Ben grabbed his rifle from the antler rack and ran outside.

Justin Miles was on his knees in his wagon on the other side of the river whipping his team into a run. A dozen Indians were strung out in a long line behind Miles. The one in front on a pinto was cutting down the distance between them at an alarming rate. He was young, no more than a boy, Ben saw, but with a rifle in his hands he was as dangerous as Jack or Sowerwick or any of the Ute braves.

As Ben ran toward the bank of the river, he thought that even Justin Miles, as lazy and worthless as he was, did not deserve to die with a Ute bullet in his back, but at this distance only a miracle shot from Ben's rifle could save him.

CHAPTER FOUR

Bucky Kregg told himself that if he never saw another potato as long as he lived it would be all right with him. Maudie had made him get out of bed before the sun was up and told him to eat breakfast and start digging potatoes. They'd put it off too long and it was feeling a little bit like snow this morning.

You didn't argue with Maudie. Nobody did except Ben Holt and he was mighty careful what he argued about. Maudie claimed she could outfight, outwork, outcuss, and outdrink any man on the river and Bucky believed her. He grinned when he thought about that no-account Justin Miles who lived on the other side of the Yampa. Maudie had him so buffaloed he ran when he saw her coming.

Bucky didn't know why he called her Maudie except that she objected to being called Grandma. She sure didn't have anything to be vain about, but she was vain about her age. She admitted that Bucky was her grandson and that he was fourteen. Anybody with a lick of sense could see she was pushing fifty and that a woman of thirty-five, which was what she claimed to be, couldn't have a grandson who was fourteen. No one challenged her though.

He put his right foot on the fork and shoved it under another hill of potatoes and lifted them out. He built a small pile at the edge of the row and went on to the next hill. They had a good crop, and with the cabbage and turnips and carrots they had raised they'd make out until spring, providing they harvested their vegetables in time and moved them into the root cellar before they had a hard freeze.

Maudie was a sight better at raising a garden than Ben Holt was, so she'd probably make the same deal with Ben she had last year, trading him garden stuff for fresh meat. Ben was a regular mountain man when it came to hunting. He could go out just about any time and come back with a deer or elk or bear and half a dozen grouse to boot.

Bucky couldn't understand how Ben did it. Bucky could take his Winchester and spend all day in the timber on either side of the river and be lucky if he brought back a rabbit. He guessed Ben had some kind of a secret he didn't aim to share with anyone.

Maybe Ben would have taken him hunting sometime, only Maudie said no. If Bucky went hunting, he went by himself. He didn't know why she was so unreasonable, and when he asked her, she told him to shut up and that was the end of it.

There were times when he thought he hated Maudie. He had shot up the last year so he was as tall as she was, but he was still a string bean, and Maudie was big and strong and could handle him any time she wanted to. If he got out of line, she made him take his pants down and she picked up the willow switch she kept in the corner and gave him a whipping. Every time she did, he promised himself it would be the last. If she tried it again he'd run away. But he never did.

He reached the end of a row and, straightening up, looked at the neat little piles of potatoes. The smart thing to do would be to sack them up and haul them into the root cellar. The clouds were hanging down low on the mountains this morning. Chances were they'd get a rain by night, or maybe a wet snow, though it probably wouldn't freeze very hard this early.

Well, he knew better than to give Maudie any suggestions once she'd made up her mind. At breakfast she'd told him to dig all the potatoes and he might just as well go ahead and dig them.

Bucky knew he was lucky for all of Maudie's faults. She was tougher than a bootheel, but he guessed anybody would be who'd lived as hard a life as Maudie had. Her husband had died when Bucky's father was a boy, but she always said she could handle anything that came along and so far she had.

Maudie raised Bucky's father. She lived alone after he was married until Bucky and his parents came down with typhoid fever. Maudie moved into their house and nursed them, but Bucky's father and mother both died. How she ever pulled Bucky through was more than he knew, and now when he got so mad at her he couldn't see straight, he remembered he'd be dead if it hadn't been for her and he'd get over his mad in a hurry.

After Bucky was well, Maudie sold her farm on the South Platte, bought tools and supplies, and loaded them into a wagon. They'd find a new place on the other side of the mountains, she told Bucky, somewhere to the west where there weren't so many people and they wouldn't have to fight things like typhoid fever.

Bucky would never forget that trip as long as he lived. They went up and down some mountain grades on shelf roads that scared him loose from his boots, but Maudie never turned a hair. After that Bucky never doubted her when she got to bragging that she could do anything a man could.

They rolled over Gore Pass on down to the Yampa. After a while Maudie stopped the team and looked around and said, 'Bucky, this is as far as we're going. If this valley wasn't right smack up against the reservation, it'd have been settled before now, so we'll grab the piece of land we want while the Utes are still here or by glory, it'll be gone.' The next morning she started building a cabin.

Bucky straightened up and looked downriver at Ben Holt's place. Ben had promised to go fishing with him, and Bucky wondered if he could sneak down to the willows along the river without Maudie seeing him. If he could get that far, he'd take off for Ben's place.

He sucked in a long breath, wondering if it

would be worth a hiding just to spend an afternoon with Ben. He wiped his forehead and decided it would be. If she was real busy with something like making bread, she wouldn't be watching him. He'd turn slow and easy as if he was resting his back by standing straight for a minute. If he didn't see her, he'd make a try for the willows.

He made the turn, slow and easy just the way he aimed to, and just about jumped out of his skin. He saw her, all right. She was standing right here in front of him, her hands on her hips, her mouth tightened into a long, grim line against her teeth.

'Just what was you thinking about, young man?' Maudie asked.

In spite of himself, he laughed. Maudie had a way of reading his mind, and he'd learned from experience that it was a mistake to lie to her. He said, 'I was thinking it would be worth a whupping to go fishing with Ben.'

She was mad or scared or something. Usually she laughed when he gave her an honest answer like that, but not this time. Her expression didn't change a bit.

'That's what I thought,' she said. 'Well, it ain't worth losing your hair. Carl Niven told me while ago that the Utes are on the warpath and they might come sashaying by here any time. He wanted us to light out for Middle Park, but I told him I wasn't walking off and leaving everything we'd done for the last two years.'

Bucky stared at her, wide-eyed, his heart pounding. He had seen Niven ride up and had watched Maudie come out of the house and talk to him, but he didn't know what the talk was about. He had seen dozens of Ute bands ride by in the two years they'd been here and the Indians had never harmed them or even threatened them. Usually they had been friendly, sometimes stopping for a meal, and on occasion Jack had left a quarter of venison for them.

The nearest thing to trouble they'd ever had was the time the fat chief Colorow had stopped and demanded something to eat. Maudie had put a meal on the table for the Indians. They had eaten everything in sight, but when Colorow rose, half a dozen biscuits fell out of his shirt to the floor.

Maudie grabbed her broom, yelling, 'I didn't think you could put so many biscuits into that big belly of yours.' She ran him out of the house, hitting him on the back with her broom every jump he made. Ben laughed so hard when she told him about it that he couldn't say a word for five minutes, then when he could talk, he said, 'I'll tell you one thing you can bank on. Colorow won't bother you again.'

'I got to worrying about it afterwards,' Maudie admitted. 'I was so mad I lost all the sense the good Lord gave me, but after he left I

31

got to thinking about what I done and I was afraid he'd come back some night and murder Bucky and me.'

Ben shook his head. 'Not Colorow. After the way you handled him, he's more scared of you than you are of him.'

Now, looking at Maudie, Bucky had a feeling she was thinking about Colorow. The talk was that he was half Comanche and he wasn't likely to forget the whacking Maudie had given him. It was all he needed to come back with a few renegades and kill both of them.

'Maybe we ought to take Niven's advice,' Bucky said uneasily.

'No, we ain't gonna run that far,' she said, 'but he told me Ben wants us to move in with him till the scare's over. Might be a good idea to do it after we take care of the potatoes. Long as it's daylight, we can see 'em coming and fight 'em off, but come dark, it'll be a different story.'

Maudie walked toward the house, turning her head to shout, 'Don't you hike off on no fishing trip. Them Injuns might be hiding in the willows right now just hankering for your scalp.'

Bucky watched her until she disappeared inside the cabin. It was the first time he had ever known her to be scared of anything, but he sensed that she was scared now. He had a hunch she would strike out for Ben's cabin this minute if she wasn't afraid someone would think she was afraid.

He wiped his forehead again, his heart slugging away inside his chest so hard it felt as if it would break loose from its moorings. He jammed the fork under the next hill of potatoes, thinking that if he worked hard he'd forget how scared he was, but it didn't help.

Bucky wasn't easily frightened, but he was plenty scared now. The notion that the Utes were just waiting down there along the river to shoot him in the back or bust his head open with a war club and then rip off his scalp was enough to give him the screaming flim-flams.

He finished with that hill and moved to the next one. Just as he lifted his foot to force the fork under the potatoes he heard the Indians yell on the other side of the river. This was the first time he'd ever heard that kind of yell, but he knew it was the Utes before he dropped the fork and started running toward the cabin. He saw them come out of the timber above the Miles cabin, eight or ten of them, a warrior on a pinto leading the charge.

Miles was hooking up his team to a wagon in front of his cabin. Bucky hadn't noticed him before, but he must have been loading up some of his things getting ready to leave. The instant Miles heard the Indians he jumped into the wagon and yelled at the team. The horses took off on the run, the wagon bouncing from one side to the other over the rough ground.

Maudie bolted out of the cabin with her Sharps rifle in her hands. Before Bucky reached the front door, Maudie knelt on one knee and took a rest on the other and pulled the trigger. The gun always sounded to Bucky like a cannon and he knew from experience how hard it kicked, but Maudie loved it.

She jumped up and threw the rifle on the ground. 'By glory,' she said angrily, 'I missed that booger on the pinto.' She watched the scene on the other side of the river, her hands fisting and closing at her sides, then she muttered, 'They're gaining on Justin. He'll never in the world make it.'

She grabbed up her Sharps and ran back into the cabin. A minute later she returned with a sack in one hand and Bucky's Winchester in the other. She said, 'I'm going to hitch up and we'll light out for Ben's place. Fill the sack with spuds. We'll take 'em along to eat. Chances are we'll be there for a spell.'

'They may come across the river after us,' Bucky called as she ran toward the barn.

'We'll blow their heads off if they do,' she shouted back, then disappeared into the barn.

He ran to the garden, a lump coming into his throat when he glanced at the cabin and thought that the Utes would probably burn it. Maudie had built it the first summer and fall they were here, with only a little help from Ben. She'd done a pretty good job, too, a better job than Justin Miles had done.

34

As soon as he reached the garden, he dropped to his knees and began scooping potatoes into the sack. He kept the Winchester beside him as he moved crab-like along the row, his head bobbing up and down as he looked toward the river and then back at the potatoes.

Every second he expected the Utes to break out of the willows and charge him, shooting and yelling like the devils they were. Then the tears started running down his cheeks and he told himself that if they got out of this, he'd never get mad at Maudie again.

CHAPTER FIVE

As Ben Holt ran toward the river, he tried to estimate the speed Justin Miles was making with his team and wagon as compared to that of the young Ute on the pinto. The Indian was riding low on his horse, a revolver in his right hand.

Although Miles was whipping his team and the mares were giving the best they had, it was impossible for a team pulling a wagon to outrun an Indian pony with a rider on his back who probably didn't weigh over one hundred and twenty pounds.

The pinto was likely one of the Utes' prize race horses. He was rapidly pulling away from the rest of the Indians and was closing the gap between him and Miles almost as rapidly. The Ute was close enough to shoot Miles in the back, but apparently he wanted to ride up beside him or get ahead of him before he fired, perhaps simply as an act of bravado.

Ben reached the east bank of the river and dropped flat on his belly. He could not risk waiting much longer, for as soon as the Indian knew he was there he'd kill Miles and wheel his horse and run.

The trouble was Ben couldn't read the Ute's mind. The Indian might decide that his victim would reach the river before he gained the position he wanted. In that case it would be simpler to shoot and run. He certainly knew there were other white families living east of the Yampa and if he kept going, he was bound to run into trouble.

The Indian was close enough now so that Ben thought he had a chance of hitting him. He cocked his Winchester, then hesitated, knowing that if he fired and missed Justin Miles would die. Then he saw the Ute level his revolver and knew he could not wait another second. He quickly brought his rifle to his shoulder, caught the Indian in his sights and squeezed off a shot.

The Ute threw up his arms, the revolver dropping from slack fingers. He spilled off his horse in a rolling fall, and when he hit the ground, he kept rolling until he reached the willows along the river and was out of Ben's sight.

The Indian wasn't dead. Apparently he hadn't been hit very hard. Still, Ben was surprised by the way he moved. He expected the fall to knock the brave's wind out of him and he'd thought he'd get another good shot at the Ute, but the Indian acted as if he hadn't even been stunned.

Hurt or not, the instinct of survival was too great to permit the Ute to lie motionless where he fell. Ben fired two more times, but he did it for the benefit of the other warriors. He couldn't see the brave he had knocked off the horse, so his bullets did nothing more than send a few willow leaves drifting to the ground.

Ben's shots turned the rest of the Ute band around in a sharp angle. Several of them fired, the bullets kicking up dirt in front of him, then they raced back toward the Miles cabin. He threw three more shots at them, but the distance was too great to do anything more than hurry them along.

Miles's mares were running hard when they hit the ford. He hadn't looked back to see whether he was being pursued or not, but was still on his knees lurching back and forth as the wagon swayed crazily behind the team. He held the lines in his right hand; he used the whip in his left as hard as he could.

The water slowed the mares, but it didn't stop them. As they pulled out on the east bank,

37

Ben got to his feet and shouted, 'You're all right, Justin. You made it.'

But Justin Miles didn't hear him. He used the whip every step the mares made, first on one and then the other. The wagon thundered past Ben, not slowing until the team reached the corral. Miles pulled the horses up and struggled to his feet and looked back. Ben ran after the wagon. When he reached it, he saw that Miles's face was ashen, his mouth was twitching, and his eyes had the glazed expression of a man who was out of his mind.

Ben saw that Miles had come close to killing the mares. Trembling, they stood spraddle-legged, their heads down, their sides heaving. Ben said, 'Go into the house, Justin. You're all right now. You're safe.'

Obediently Miles swung to the ground. Cherry ran toward them from the house, calling, 'Is he all right, Ben?'

'He will be when he gets over his scare,' Ben said. 'Take him inside. You'll find a bottle of whisky in the kitchen. He looks like he could use a jolt.'

Without a word Cherry took her father's arm and led him into the house. He went with her like a child, his eyes still glazed. The thought occurred to Ben that Miles might never recover his senses. He had heard of cases like this in which men had been so thoroughly frightened that they had become insane or reduced to a state of infantile mentality.

He took a good deal of time with the mares, walking them and rubbing them down, and when he finally tied them in the back stalls of his barn, he wasn't sure whether they would ever be any good again or not. As he strode across the yard, he saw a column of smoke upstream on the other side of the river. The Utes had fired the Miles cabin.

When Ben went into the house, he found Justin Miles sitting in a chair in front of the fireplace. He was still in a daze, not turning his head to look at Ben when he came in, or answering when Ben spoke to him. Cherry stepped out of the kitchen when she heard Ben and motioned for him to join her.

When he stepped into the kitchen, she closed the door. She said, 'I never saw him act like this before. He just sits there staring at nothing. He won't say a word. He wouldn't even put his hand out to take the drink of whisky I offered. In all my life I never knew him to turn down a drink of whisky.'

'He got a bad scare,' Ben said. 'Looks to me like he doesn't even know he's alive.'

'Well, he might just as well be dead as to be this way,' she said.

'I'll cut off them venison steaks.' He picked up a butcher knife from the table. 'No use to cook anything for Justin, looks like.'

'I don't think there is.' When Ben reached the back door, she asked, 'Shouldn't one of us keep a lookout for the Indians? They might

39

cross the river.'

He shook his head. 'Not right away they won't,' he said. 'Looks like they've burned your cabin. The barn, too, probably. At least that's the way it looked from the smoke. They'll amuse themselves around there for a while.'

'Well, I don't suppose Pa will ever get around to building again even if he comes out of this,' she said. 'I guess there's nothing to go back to, and in a way I'm glad.'

'You've got a home here,' he said. 'We didn't quite get that settled.'

'It's settled,' she said, smiling. 'That is, if you still want me. Funny how a person's ideas can be changed. It didn't take me more'n a minute when I was watching the Indians chase Pa and I saw you go down there to the river to risk your life to save a man who's hated you and didn't deserve anything from you. It was almost like hearing a voice. All of a sudden I knew how important it was to be alive. It didn't make any sense to go on taking care of Pa and ... and ...'

She stopped, her face flushed with embarrassment. He laid the butcher knife on the table and walked to her. 'Honey, are you saying in a roundabout way that you'll marry me?'

'Oh yes, Ben,' she said. 'I've admired and respected you from the moment I first met you. I've told myself that a woman would be lucky to be your wife because you're not afraid of anything and you have a way of making other people not be afraid because you're not.'

He took her hands and opened his mouth to say something, but before he could say a word, she said, 'I love you, Ben. I've loved you all the time. I was afraid to let you know because of Pa. Maybe he'll be worse now that this has happened, but then maybe we won't live through the Indian war, either. I wanted you to know.'

He put his arms around her and hugged her hard, then he kissed her. He said, 'Cherry, we'll get married as soon as we can find a preacher and we'll have a whole passel of children and we'll work hard. Most of all, we're going to be happy.'

'I know we are, Ben.' she said.

He kissed her again, but it seemed they had barely started when they heard the creak of a wagon, and Maudie Kregg's bellow, 'You in there, Ben?'

'Oh, drat,' Cherry said.

Ben winked at her and went outside, seeing that Justin Miles had not moved. When Maudie saw him, she asked, 'How'd you make out with old man Miles? I heard some shooting and before that I seen that wolf pack chasing him like they was the devil's own spawn. There was too much brush in the way to see how it turned out.'

'He's alive,' Ben said, 'but he don't seem to know what's going on.'

41

'Was he hurt?' Maudie demanded. 'Did that Injun on the pinto shoot him?'

Ben shook his head. 'Near as I can figure it, he's just scared. I guess he thought he was gonna get killed, so he just sits staring at the wall without knowing what's going on around him.'

Maudie snorted in disgust. 'Now ain't that just what you'd expect from a no-account piece of male flesh like him.'

'Cherry's in the house,' Ben said. 'She was fixing to cook dinner, but I didn't get around to cutting off the venison steaks. That quarter I've got is still on the pole.'

Maudie handed the lines to Bucky and got down. Ben almost grinned. Anything Maudie did from getting out of a wagon seat to plowing a field or cooking a meal was performed with grim determination.

'I'll take care of it,' she said. 'You show Bucky where you want him to put the horses.' She lifted the sack of potatoes from the wagon box. 'I didn't ask you, Ben, but maybe I orter. We're moving in with you, me'n Bucky, and all we fetched to throw into the pot is a sack of spuds.'

This time Ben did grin. She wasn't asking; she was telling him. 'Sure, Maudie, if you can share the kitchen with Cherry and not boss her around.'

Maudie put the sack on the ground and placed both hands on her hips. 'Ben Holt, I can

42

and will share the same kitchen with Cherry, but glory to hell, of course I'll boss her around and you know it.'

'Well, try to go easy on her,' Ben said. 'Maybe it won't surprise you none, but we'll be getting married before long.'

'Congratulations,' Maudie said, 'and I sure ain't surprised one bit. You're getting a fine girl, once you separate her from her no-good pa.'

'That'll be a problem if he don't come out of it,' Ben admitted.

Maudie picked up the potatoes, hesitated, then she said, 'Ben, you know I ain't afraid of the dark or the devil or grizzly bears, and when Carl Niven stopped and told me about the Injuns, I said I was gonna hang tight with Bucky and we'd defend our buildings come hell or high water, but you know something? When I seen them ornery devils take out after old Justin while ago, I said to myself that the damned buildings wasn't worth it, so here we are. My Sharps and Bucky's Winchester are in the wagon along with all the shells we've got.'

'I'm glad you're here,' Ben said. 'With you two, I figure we can hold off a purty good-sized band of Indians.'

'Sure we can,' Maudie said and, turning, strode into the house, the sack of potatoes on her shoulder.

'Drive to the barn,' Ben said. 'We'll leave the wagon beside Justin's and put your horses into

43

the corral.'

'Yes sir.' Bucky swallowed, opened his mouth and closed it and swallowed again, then he blurted, 'Ben, a good man don't get scared of things, does he?'

'Depends,' Ben answered. 'Sometimes honest fear makes a man real careful and helps him stay alive.'

'I'm sure gonna be careful,' Bucky said. 'I don't get scared easy, but thinking about them Injuns and the way they scalp folks and cut 'em up and stuff, well, it just gave me the shakes.'

'It's nothing to be ashamed of,' Ben said.

Bucky gave him a grateful glance. 'Thanks, Ben. If it comes to a fight, I'll do my share.'

'I know you will,' Ben said, and thought that compared to Justin Miles, Bucky Kregg was a full-grown man.

CHAPTER FIVE

When they finished eating, Ben leaned back in his chair and patted his stomach. 'A good dinner, Cherry,' he said. 'That venison steak sure tasted better'n any I ever cooked.'

'Yeah, it sure was good,' Bucky agreed.

'Hell's bells and kitten britches,' Maudie shouted. 'I fried them steaks. Cherry baked the biscuits and peeled the potatoes and I . . .' She stopped and glared at Ben who was grinning

44

broadly. 'I know a certain joker who's gonna go hungry one of these days.'

'She's right,' Cherry said uneasily. 'All I did was...'

'Never mind him, honey.' Maudie patted the girl's shoulder. 'I don't know why I always bite when he sets a trap for me. I knew he was hoorawing me the minute I started blowing off.'

'Sure, I was just funnin',' Ben said. 'It don't make no difference who cooked what. I say it was a good meal.'

Maudie grumbled something under her breath, then she said, 'Ben, I want to know what you're aiming to do. Justin ain't gonna be much help, sitting in a chair like he was in a stupor, but there's four of us who can shoot. You fetched in your Winchester and my Sharps, Bucky?'

'Yeah, and the shells, too,' the boy answered.

'You've got an old Henry besides your Winchester, don't you, Ben?' Maudie asked.

He nodded. 'Still shoots purty good, too. I've got plenty of shells for both rifles. Likewise I've got a Colt .45 hanging from the antlers there by the door. We're pretty well fixed if it comes to a siege.'

'You figure it will?' Maudie asked uneasily.

Ben shrugged. 'Maudie, you know you can't outguess an Indian. We've had an hour or two being able to relax and enjoy ourselves, but by

45

this time they're probably done playing around Justin's cabin and barn, so from now on we'd better keep a guard outside all the time to holler if the Indians show themselves. Bucky, I guess you can be the first. I'll take your place after while.'

Bucky rose. 'Want me to stay in front of the house?'

'Oh, you might sashay over to the barn once in a while,' Ben said. 'Keep an eye on the back of the house, too. I think they'll stay along the river, but there's no way to be sure. All we know is that they're mighty tricky.'

Bucky picked up his Winchester that he had left by the front door and went outside. When Ben was sure he was out of earshot, he leaned forward and said in a low tone, 'I didn't want to worry Bucky, but I guess we're old enough to face facts. We're in a hell of a tight spot. It'll be days before any help comes from Fort Steele and this bunch that chased Justin is bound to get bigger. From what I could see of 'em, they're young bucks not much more'n kids. Chances are they got bored sitting around and firing at the soldiers, so they rode off looking for excitement.'

'I guess they found some,' Cherry said.

'They'll find some more, too,' Ben went on. 'You can count on it, but it's hard to figure out how they'll go at it. They may cross the river and burn you out, Maudie. That'd be some safe excitement. They might try to steal our horses. Or maybe they'll just hide in the willows and knock us off one at a time.'

Maudie scowled and nodded as if that was about the way she sized it up. She said, 'I ain't sure we done right leaving home. I don't cotton to the notion of starting all over again. I don't have no more money, neither.'

'I'm in the same boat,' Ben told her, 'but the way I look at it, we've got a good chance of getting through this alive if we're together, but we'll probably go under if you and Bucky stay at your place and there's just me'n Cherry here. So, if we defend my house and you lose yours, it'd be only fair for me to help you if they burn you out.'

Maudie heaved a great sigh. 'That takes a burden off my shoulders, though I guess I knew that was what you'd say. Maybe it won't be that bad. Them red devils may light out for Hayden or Steamboat Springs and we might not have no more trouble with 'em.'

It wouldn't work that way, Ben thought, but he didn't want to worry Cherry any more than she was already, so he shrugged and said, 'One thing's sure. This bunch or another one like it will take a whack at Hank Long's trading post.'

'They've got plenty of reason to hate him,' Maudie said. 'I wouldn't blame 'em if they took that booger's clothes off and staked him out over an ant hill.'

'Either way,' Ben said, 'we've got to figure

out what we're going to do. The first thing is to work out a scheme so at least one of us will be on the lookout all the time. Maudie, you might spell him off till it's time to cook supper...'

'Ben, somebody's coming,' Bucky called from the doorway. Ben jumped up and ran to a window. Three riders were coming along the road from Maudie's place, two men and a woman. Ben wasn't sure whether the woman was grown or a child. She was very small, and at this distance he couldn't be sure.

'I'll talk to 'em,' Ben said. 'I guess we can't let 'em go on. They'd be easy pickings for the Indians.'

'I'll go with you,' Maudie grumbled. 'Cherry, clean off the table. We'll have to feed 'em. First thing you know, Ben, you'll be running a hotel.'

'We'll be hungry before long if that happens,' Ben said. 'I don't have enough grub to feed a lot of people.'

As he crossed the living room to the front door, Ben saw that Justin Miles had left the chair where he'd been sitting and was sprawled on the couch, apparently asleep. He'd probably be all right when he woke up, Ben thought, as he took his Winchester down from the antlers.

'Justin is faking,' Maudie said in disgust. 'This way he won't have to do no fighting. He won't even have to take his turn doing guard duty.'

'In that case he won't eat,' Ben said as he stepped outside.

Maudie caught up her Sharps and followed Ben. She said in a low tone, 'I wanted him to hear that. When he gets hungry, he'll come out of it and I figure he'd better decide right now whether he wants to go hungry or start being a man.'

Ben was only half listening, his gaze on the three riders. They were close enough for Ben to see that the man in front was older than the other two, probably about thirty. He was well-built, a good-looking man who wore a broad-brimmed, black hat and a Prince Albert coat.

The other two were kids. The boy was about eighteen, big and raw-boned and rough-featured. The girl was younger, although Ben saw that she was not the child he had thought she might be. He guessed she was sixteen, and he wondered what they were doing out here in a wild country like this.

The older man dismounted and, taking off his hat, bowed in Maudie's direction. 'I'm David Wheeler from Greeley.' He offered his hand to Ben. 'We are relieved to find someone. The place above here was deserted.'

'I'm Ben Holt.' Ben liked Wheeler's hard grip, the direct way the gray eyes met his. 'This is Mrs Maudie Kregg. The place you just passed belongs to her. She's holed up with us because we've got a better chance of getting through this Indian trouble alive if we fight together than if we fight alone.'

'That makes good sense.' Wheeler introduced the other two who were standing on the ground beside their horses; the girl's face showing her fatigue. They were Mr and Mrs Bradley, Wheeler said, and added, 'We met on the trail last night. This morning we met a man on the trail who told us about the uprising. He said we should turn back to Middle Park, but we weren't sure the report was true. Besides, we felt it was about as dangerous to turn back as it was to go on.'

'I ain't afraid of no Injuns,' Bradley said, his voice loud and overbearing. 'If I had a gun, I'd send the whole bunch back to the reservation, but we didn't have no gun.'

Maudie took a long breath, her gaze on young Bradley's face. 'So you ain't afraid of no Injuns. Well sir, I guess that makes you about the bravest man on the Yampa.'

Wheeler sensed Maudie's indignation. Bradley's insolent remark had made cowards out of all of them, so Wheeler gestured toward the Continental Divide, the peaks still hidden by a heavy cloud cover. He said, 'When we rode down to where we could see the valley, we watched a band of Indians chase a man in a wagon, so of course we knew the report of the uprising was true. Did they kill him?'

'He got away, but it was close.' Ben looked at the girl, seeing that she was tired and dirty and she might even be sick. He brought his

50

gaze back to Wheeler. 'You didn't intend to go on, did you?'

'It depends on whether you'll let us stay.' Wheeler glanced at the Bradleys, hesitated, then said, 'Melissa is all in. We would be thankful if we could stay here till the trouble's over.'

'Like I said, we wouldn't be worried none if we had a gun,' Bradley said, 'but we'd be setting ducks if them Injuns caught up with us.'

'You men take care of the horses,' Maudie said. 'Mrs Bradley, you come into the house with me. I reckon you folks ain't et, have you?'

Wheeler smiled. 'Mrs Kregg, we haven't had a good meal for a long time.'

'We'll fill your bellies up good.' Maudie put an arm around Melissa. 'Young man, don't look to me like you take care of your wife very well.'

'Oh, Rick takes care of me real good,' Melissa said defensively. 'I'm just a little tired. Kind of scared, too.'

'You got a right to be, honey,' Maudie said. 'We don't like to admit it, but we're all scared ever since they gave Justin Miles the run they did this morning.' She glared at Rick, then she added, 'Chances are most of them Utes are watching us right now from the willows yonder. Here, take my Sharps and run 'em back to the reservation.'

'No,' Melissa cried. 'I don't want Rick to get killed. Mrs Kregg, sometimes he just talks

51

too much.'

'Yeah, I guess he does,' Maudie said, 'but around here you either put up or keep your damned mouth shut. As far as I'm concerned, you two men are the biggest fools I ever seen to travel in this country without no guns.'

Maudie strode into the house, dragging Melissa with her. The girl looked back at her husband as if she could not bear being parted from him for even a few minutes. How she could love a loud-mouthed braggart like Rick Bradley was more than Ben could figure out, but he had learned long ago that it was foolish to try to understand why women loved the men they did.

Wheeler laughed softly as he watched Maudie and Melissa until they disappeared inside the house. Then he said, 'There goes a strong woman.'

'She's an old bitch,' Bradley said angrily. 'She's just like Melissa's mother. She didn't have no right to say what she did.'

'She had plenty of right,' Ben said in disgust, 'after listening to you run off at the mouth.'

Bradley stood three inches taller than Ben, his shoulders were wider, and his hands tightened into huge fists as he glared angrily at Ben.

'We'd better put our horses up,' Wheeler said quickly. 'We'll all feel better when we get that meal Mrs Kregg promised us.'

Ben turned on his heels and strode to the

corral, jerking his head for the two men to follow him. He'd give young Bradley his Henry rifle and send him on down the river if it wasn't for the girl, he told himself, and knew at once he wouldn't.

He waited as the two men stripped gear from the three horses, Wheeler taking care of Melissa's mount. As soon as they were watered and turned into the corral, Ben told the men to feed them from the nearest haystack.

Ben watched, wondering how many more people he would have to put up before the Indian scare was over. He had enough hay in the stacks to get his three horses and his small herd of cattle through the winter and maybe have a little to spare, but if this kept up, he'd be short and he didn't have any money to buy more.

When the two men finished and came toward him, Wheeler said, 'Rick, you go on into the house and see how Melissa's getting along. I'll be in soon as I talk to Mr Holt for a minute.'

Bradley wheeled away without a word and crossed the yard to the house in a leggy, adolescent stride. Ben, watching him, said, 'About all that kid's got is a big mouth. What business has he got with a wife?'

'None,' Wheeler admitted, 'but they ran away from home to get married, or so they told me. They aim to buy a ranch somewhere on the Yampa where they figure their folks won't find them.'

'Buy a ranch?' Ben asked incredulously. 'What would a kid like that use for money?'

'I've asked myself the same question,' Wheeler said gravely. 'The first answer you think of is that they stole it when they left home. The running away part I can believe. I'm not so sure about stealing the money. They don't strike me as being thieves. Not Melissa anyhow.'

'We get all kinds out here,' Ben said thoughtfully. 'A lot of 'em are men who done something back in civilization and they come out here in the wilderness to forget it.'

'I'm afraid you're right,' Wheeler said, 'but the frontier is a place where men can start over without being asked any questions. Mostly they're men who can look out for themselves. Rick Bradley couldn't make it through the first winter without help. Neither could Melissa.'

Ben grinned. 'By the time Maudie gets done with 'em, they'll be willing to head back home.'

'Rick would have gone before now, but Melissa wouldn't let him. She's got enough steel in her backbone for both of them.' Wheeler hesitated, his eyes on the willows along the river. 'You say the Indians are hiding down there now?'

'I'm not sure, but the chances are they're watching us,' Ben said. 'They haven't shot at us and I doubt that they will, but about the time we think they won't bother us they'll make a try for our horses.'

'It's too bad,' Wheeler said. 'I'm from Greeley and I know Nathan Meeker and his wife and daughter Josie. I admire them for their idealism. You see, I'm a preacher and I gave up my church to come here and help Nathan at the agency. He was in Greeley earlier this year, you know, and I had a long talk with him. I was much impressed by his long-range program and his plans for developing the natural resources the Utes have on their reservation.'

'His program would never have worked,' Ben said harshly. 'I know him, too. He's not a practical man. He never learned to deal with the Utes. You don't run before you walk if you're a child, and these White River Utes are children. Savages, sure, and they can be mean like the ones who were chasing Justin Miles this morning, but if Meeker had handled them right, the meanness might never have come out.'

Wheeler considered what Ben said, then he took his hat off and ran his hand through his hair. 'I know most of the boys that Nathan hired the last time he was in Greeley. What do you think is the situation at the agency now?'

'I hate to say it, but the odds are ninety-nine to one that Meeker and the rest of the whites have been massacred. The Utes hated him. There were a lot of reasons, but one was that he tried to make them get rid of some of their horses. He even plowed up a lot of their pasture. So, after they attacked the soldiers who never should have come in the first place, it don't look to me like the whites at the agency had a chance.'

Maudie called from the front door, 'Come and get it before I throw it out to the coyotes.'

Wheeler fell into step with Ben as they walked toward the house. He said glumly, 'I guess I should have stayed in Greeley. I knew the whites at the agency would want to hear the word preached, but it's apparent I can do nothing for the Indians.'

'You can do something for yourself,' Ben said. 'You can stay alive.'

Wheeler glanced again at the willows as if expecting to see the Indians who were hiding there. Then he said, 'Yes, I guess that's the problem that faces all of us.'

'The valley will be settled as soon as the Utes are moved out of Colorado,' Ben said. 'That's bound to happen after this. We need a preacher.'

'Well then,' Wheeler said as if relieved. 'I'll figure out some way to make a living. I'd like to live here.'

CHAPTER SEVEN

Cherry had cleared the table and was washing the dishes when Maudie brought Melissa Bradley into the kitchen. Maudie introduced Cherry to the girl, then said, 'You sit right down and rest. You look as peaked as if you'd been drug through a knothole.'

'I'm ... I'm all right, Mrs Kregg,' Melissa protested, but she dropped into the chair that Maudie offered without argument.

Maudie turned to the doorway that opened into the living room and called, 'Bucky, come here.'

The boy obeyed, staring curiously at Melissa. Maudie introduced them, then she said, 'I've got a chore for you. I want you to fill the reservoir on the back of the stove, then fill the tea kettle and after that bring in the boiler off the back porch and fill it.'

Bucky stared at her. 'What're you fixing to do, Maudie? You gonna take a bath?'

'No, but Melissa is,' Maudie said. 'She's been riding and camping out till she's just plain dirty. When you get done, fill both buckets and leave 'em on the floor there by the stove.'

'With all that water, I figured it'd be you taking the bath,' Bucky grumbled.

Maudie made a swipe at him with her hand as he crossed the kitchen to the back door. He

57

ducked it easily as he went on out of the house. Maudie grunted, 'He's a smart-aleck. That's what he is.'

Cherry smiled as she glanced at Maudie. 'He's a good boy and you're proud of him.'

'Yeah, I reckon I am,' Maudie admitted, 'but I sure wouldn't let him know it. Well, I'll go cut some venison.'

'Please don't bother with me,' Melissa said. 'I know I'm dirty, but we ran away from home and got married. We were afraid our folks would try to make us come home, so we've been riding as fast as we could.'

'Riding fast don't give you no excuse for getting as dirty as you are,' Maudie said. 'Of course I'll bother. You'll have to sleep with Cherry in Mr Holt's bed tonight, and Cherry sure don't want to sleep with no dirty girl.'

Maudie picked up the butcher knife and sailed out of the kitchen. Bucky brought in two buckets of water and filled the reservoir, then went back to the pump with the tea kettle. Melissa sat with her head down and Cherry thought she was crying. She went to the girl as soon as she finished drying the dishes and put an arm around her.

'Don't mind her, Melissa,' Cherry said. 'She runs roughshod over all of us and nobody stands up to her, but she means well.'

'I'll stand up to her.' Melissa raised her head to look at Cherry. 'She's just like my mother. I didn't come out here to be bossed around by no

58

big woman like her. I'm not going to take a bath and I'm going to sleep with Rick tonight. A wife belongs with her husband.'

Cherry drew her arm back and straightened up, realizing that Melissa had been sulking instead of crying. 'You'll have to take orders the same as Bucky and I do. We're all in danger as long as the Indians are around. Mr Holt will tell us what to do.'

'With Mrs Kregg's help,' Melissa said.

Cherry laughed. 'Oh, Maudie will help, all right, but what I'm saying is that us women will sleep inside and the men will sleep outside. They won't come into the house unless the Indians attack us. None of us can do just what we want to do at a time like this.'

Melissa stared defiantly at Cherry. 'I'm going to sleep with Rick tonight.'

Irritated, Cherry said, 'I'm sorry, Melissa, but if you're going to stay here, you'll take orders. If you won't take them, you and your husband will have to ride on, and the chances are you won't go a mile before you're both killed by the Utes.'

Cherry returned to the work table at the window and began stirring up a batch of biscuits. Bucky came in with the tea kettle and set it on the stove, then returned to the pump. Cherry remained facing the window, her back to Melissa. In a way she sympathized with the girl.

Melissa was tired and hungry and frail, but

59

her stubborn defiance was no way to handle her problem. Maudie would make her toe the mark, by force if necessary, but the result might be that Melissa in a fit of anger would persuade her husband to go on regardless of the danger.

Melissa, who had been looking through the window, watched Maudie bring the meat down from the top of the pole, slice off three thick steaks, wrap the remainder, and run it back up. She asked, 'Why do you keep meat on a pole that way?'

'Two reasons,' Cherry answered. 'Number one, Ben doesn't have a cooler or an ice house, and the meat won't keep inside this time of year. Number two, the animals can't get at it on the pole.'

'I never heard of such a thing,' Melissa said.

Bucky came in with two buckets of water and emptied them into the big copper boiler he had set on the back of the stove. He went back to the pump and Maudie came in with the venison. She started it frying, placed the coffee pot on the front of the stove, and helped Cherry peel the potatoes. She was filling the firebox with wood when Rick Bradley came into the kitchen.

'We're almost out of wood, Mister Bradley,' Maudie said. 'You'll find a bucksaw out back and plenty of wood that Mr Holt hauled in for the winter, so get busy.'

Rick was affronted. 'I just came in to see

how Melissa was.'

'She's gonna be fine,' Maudie said, 'and we sure don't need you underfoot while we're fixing your dinner. I'll call you soon as it's ready.'

Still he stood there, glancing at Melissa who reached out and took his hand. He was big and awkward and, Cherry suspected, very lazy. For a moment he glared at Maudie like a petulant child, then he burst out, 'I'll fight Indians all day, but it's Holt's job to cut his own wood.'

For a moment Cherry thought Maudie was going to slap the boy's face. When she had brought her temper under control, she said, 'You'll work, boy, or you won't eat. Now get out there before I kick your tail through the door.'

'Go on, Rick,' Melissa murmured. 'You're going to have to work for our dinner.'

Bradley shrugged his beefy shoulders and stomped out through the back door. A moment later as Cherry set the table she heard the tired sound of the saw as Bradley pushed and pulled it back and forth across the pine log.

Maudie didn't say another word until the meal was ready, then she called David Wheeler into the kitchen. She introduced him to Cherry, and after he had washed and combed his hair, she stepped to the back door and yelled at Bradley.

'Grub's ready,' Maudie called. 'Fetch the wood with you.'

When Bradley came in, he carried a small armload which he dropped into the woodbox at the end of the stove. He sat down at the table without washing and fidgeted impatiently until Wheeler finished asking a blessing, then he started to eat as if he were famished.

Ben came into the kitchen and sent Bucky outside to watch for Indians. Cherry moved to where Ben stood with his back to the wall and took his hand. He looked at her and winked and she smiled at him, feeling a peace within herself that was wonderful and surprising. She wished they could be alone, but there was little chance of that as long as these people were here.

Bradley looked up from his plate and pinned his gaze on Maudie. 'How much do you want for your farm?'

She stared at him for a moment, her lips parted as if this was the most surprising question she had ever heard. She drew in a long, ragged breath and said, 'I don't want to sell.'

'Sure you do,' Bradley said as if her answer was ridiculous. 'The thing you've got to decide is whether you want to take what me'n Melissa can pay.'

'Sonny, I'll say this as loud and clear as I can,' Maudie bellowed. 'We don't want to sell. Bucky and me have put a lot of sweat and work into that farm, and the Lord willing, I'll live out my years there if the Injuns don't burn us out.'

'Put a price on it,' Bradley said doggedly. 'That's the only way to settle a proposition like this.'

Maudie took another long breath. Cherry thought she was going to explode, and she probably would have if David Wheeler hadn't said in a mild voice, 'She doesn't want to sell, Rick.'

'That's right, Mister Bradley,' Maudie roared. 'I do not want to sell.'

Bradley shrugged and let it go at that. Cherry squeezed Ben's hand, her gaze on David Wheeler's face. This was a crazy situation; the two kids who were uninvited guests were going to drive Maudie wild. Wheeler was probably the only one who could handle them.

Funny, Cherry thought, how she felt toward people when she first met them. She had disliked Rick Bradley the moment she set eyes on him, but it was different with Wheeler. He was mild-mannered, but she sensed a great strength in him she had never sensed in any other man except Ben and that was because she knew him. Now, thinking about the quiet way he handled Rick Bradley, she decided he was an expert at using a gentle persuasion that was hard to deny.

When the three people finished eating, Maudie said briskly, 'Now you men clear out. We're doing the dishes and Melissa's taking a bath. Ben, we need more wood. That'll give you something to do, but we'll feel better if you don't go away.'

'We'll be on hand if you need us,' Ben said.

'Thanks for a very good meal,' Wheeler said.

Maudie smiled, pleased. 'Why now, you sure are welcome.' She jerked a thumb at the back door. 'Git now, all of you.'

'We're going,' Ben said. 'You've got us scared.'

Maudie chuckled as Ben closed the back door. 'Keep 'em scared. I always say. Men will take advantage of you if you don't.'

'You don't scare Ben,' Cherry said. 'I don't think anything scares him very much, not even the Indians.'

'He's scared just enough to be cautious,' Maudie said, 'and that's the way it ought to be. He's a good man, Cherry. You're lucky to be getting him. Well now, let's get these dishes cleaned up and we'll give Melissa her bath.'

'I'm not a baby, Mrs Kregg,' Melissa cried. 'I can bathe myself.'

'Sure you can, honey,' Maudie said, 'but I aim to do some scrubbing. Cherry will wash your clothes while you're taking the bath, then you sit by the fire till they dry. You'll feel a lot better. That yaller hair of yours will be right purty when we get it cleaned up or I miss my guess.'

Melissa looked at Cherry as if to ask how you fought off an avalanche or a flood or

64

Maudie Kregg. Cherry winked at her, trying to tell her you didn't fight Maudie off. You just went along with her.

As soon as the dishes were done. Maudie mixed the hot and cold water in the tub, then she said, 'Off with your clothes, Melissa.'

The girl hesitated, then sighed and began unbuttoning her dress. Maudie tossed each grimy garment to Cherry as Melissa took them off, the knee-length drawers coming last. When she finally stood naked beside the stove, Cherry thought she had never seen anyone as skinny and frail as this girl. Melissa put her hands over her tiny, pointed breasts, glancing at Cherry as if embarrassed, so Cherry turned her back and began washing her clothes.

'That's a bad sore you've got on your hip,' Maudie said. 'How'd you get it?'

'I bruised it before I left home,' Melissa said. 'I keep bumping it so it gets worse all the time.'

'Ben's got some salve that'll help,' Maudie said. 'I'll get it soon as we're done.' She started rubbing soap on a rag, then she stopped and stared at Melissa's back. 'Cherry,' she breathed. 'Look at this girl's back. I never seen anything like it. What in the world happened to you?'

Cherry wiped her hands on her apron and stepped to the tub. She gasped. Red, hideous scars covered the girl's back. For a moment Melissa hesitated as if ashamed to tell how she'd got them, then she said in a low tone, 'My

65

mother whipped me.'

'Oh honey,' Maudie whispered. 'I've been saying to myself that you were a fool to leave home and marry a boy who can't take care of you, but I had no idea. I guess anything would be better than living in the kind of home you had.'

Maudie threw her arms around the girl and hugged her, and suddenly Melissa began to cry. For the first time since Cherry had known Maudie, she saw the big woman cry, too. Cherry kept her back to them as she finished washing Melissa's clothes. A great lump came into her throat and she realized that tears were running down her cheeks.

Maudie had a tough hide, but Ben was right about her. She had a heart as big as her two feet put together. If anyone could do something for Melissa, Maudie could.

CHAPTER EIGHT

Ben and David Wheeler took turns with the saw, the other splitting the blocks of pine with the ax. Wheeler had taken off his coat and rolled up his sleeves, and Ben, looking at him, thought he had never seen harder muscled forearms on a man.

Wheeler swung the ax with precision. and when he had the saw, he made it sing, the yellow sawdust piling up on both sides of the log. He stopped occasionally to talk, but he was never out of breath.

Once as they changed, Ben said, 'You don't work like any preacher I ever seen. I don't have nothing against preachers, but . . .' He stopped, realizing he wasn't saying this very well, and blurted, 'I mean, a blind man could see you're an expert with an ax and a saw.'

Wheeler didn't say anything for a moment. He sank the ax blade into the chopping block and straightened up, then he remarked, 'I've worked with them some,' and let it go at that. He looked at the peaks to the east that were still shrouded by heavy clouds. The afternoon had not warmed up, and the air was still damp and carried the promise of rain or a wet snow.

Wheeler nodded at Rick Bradley who was piling stove sticks against the side of the house with slow, deliberate motions. He said in a low tone, 'Strikes me that Rick isn't much good here. Maybe he could help Bucky watch for Indians.'

Ben nodded. He had given the saw to Bradley just once. After watching the boy's slow movements for a minute, he had taken the saw back and told Bradley to spell Wheeler off with the ax. That hadn't lasted more than a minute either.

The boy missed the block completely the first time and almost missed it the second, barely chipping off a sliver of bark. He finally succeeded in splitting it, then he ran into a sizeable knot when he'd tried to cut the half block into stove wood size. His ax stuck in the chunk, so he kept pounding it against the chopping block until the knot snapped loudly and one piece of wood sailed past Ben's head, missing him by inches. Wheeler took the ax again and Ben ordered Bradley to carry the stove wood to the back of the house and pile it beside the steps.

Now, when Bradley returned from carrying an armload of wood to the house, Ben said, 'We'd better have somebody besides Bucky watching out for the Indians. Go around to the front door and get my Henry and go to the barn. You can watch from there.'

Bradley stared at Ben in his insolent way. 'Maybe I'd rather watch from the house.'

'And maybe you'll do what I tell you or you'd better get started on down the river,' Ben snapped. 'If there's trouble, it'll come at the barn because the Utes will be trying for our horses.'

'Then let the kid take the barn and I'll watch from the house,' Bradley said.

Ben's hands trembled at his sides. He bit his lower lip, holding back the hot words that threatened to spill out of him. Now even Wheeler's patience had come to an end. He said, 'Rick, I think you'd better saddle up and get out, but don't try to take Melissa.'

'Why not?' Bradley demanded. 'She's my

68

wife, ain't she?'

'I don't know about that,' Wheeler said. 'All I know is that it's time you started acting like a husband.'

For a moment Bradley's gaze was fixed on Ben's face, a wild, almost animal-like hatred in his eyes, then he muttered, 'All right, all right,' and wheeled and strode around the corner of the house.

'I'm going to break that kid's neck if he stays around here,' Ben said.

'I wouldn't blame you,' Wheeler said. 'I haven't had a good chance to talk with Melissa, but you wonder why she ever took up with a boy like that.' He hesitated, then he added, 'I think you'd better watch him. He resents taking orders from anyone.'

'I'll watch him, all right,' Ben said. 'He's not just ornery. He's a fool. He tried to buy Maudie's place, but he'd starve to death on a ranch.'

'I'm afraid so,' Wheeler agreed. 'I haven't seen him do anything right yet.'

Wheeler picked up the ax and began to work. Ben turned back to the saw, his thoughts still on Rick Bradley. It wasn't enough to have to worry about what the Indians were going to do. He had to be stuck with an obnoxious, ungrateful kid.

They worked until the sun was almost down. Maudie came out of the house, saying that supper would be ready soon and they'd better take care of the horses. She looked at the pile of stove wood next to the house and guessed they'd worked up enough to last as long as the Indian scare did.

Maudie hesitated, scratching a mole on her chin. It held four black whiskers that bristled belligerently when she was worked up about something. They bristled now.

'I put Melissa to bed in your room, Ben,' Maudie said. 'I figured Cherry could sleep with her and I'll sleep on the couch that Justin's been keeping warm all day. I reckon you men will sleep in the barn?'

Ben nodded. 'Except for the guards. How's Justin?'

'He's right as rain,' Maudie said in disgust. 'Don't you let him fool you into thinking anything else.' She scratched the mole again, then she said, 'I sure feel sorry for Melissa. She's just a child, but here she is, married to that no-good kid. I aim to let her sleep till morning and I don't propose to let the boy bother her.'

'Of course not,' Ben said. 'He'll be in the barn with the rest of us. He'll take his turn at standing guard, too.'

'Just one thing,' Wheeler said. 'Melissa is a sort of balance wheel that controls Rick. I don't know what he'll do without her. Sometimes I think he's not entirely rational.'

Maudie glared at Wheeler. 'You gonna buck me on this?'

70

'No,' Wheeler said. 'It's just that we have to recognize that Melissa is a stable girl, but Rick isn't a responsible boy. I don't know what to expect from him. I can't see why Melissa ran away from home to marry him. She jumped from the frying pan into the fire, seems to me.'

'She had reason to leave home,' Maudie said darkly. She turned and lumbered toward the back door, calling back, 'Don't forget. Supper's about ready.'

Wheeler leaned the ax against the chopping block. 'I guess we'd better go do what she says. I didn't have any intention of bucking her. I hope she knows that.'

Ben laughed. 'I'm sure she does. I don't suppose she ever seriously considers the possibility that any man would buck her.'

They walked around the house to the barn, finding Bucky where he was supposed to be but Rick Bradley wasn't in sight. They circled the corral and found him asleep, the Henry rifle on the ground beside him, his hat over his eyes.

A savage fury roared through Ben as he stared at the sleeping boy. He yelled, 'Here they come. Run for the house.'

Bradley came up off the ground in one enormous leap. He picked up the rifle, shouting, 'Where are they? I'll stop 'em.'

He faced the river and began firing wildly. Ben jerked the rifle out of his hand. 'Don't waste any more ammunition. I haven't seen any Indians.'

71

Bradley ran a hand over his face and shook his head. Puzzled, he stared at Ben. He asked, 'Why did you say they were coming?'

'Because you were asleep on your job,' Ben said harshly. 'I ought to beat hell out of you. If you were in the army, you'd be shot for going to sleep on guard duty. We might all have been killed because of your negligence.'

Bradley blinked, and then the truth hit him. He started to curse Ben, shouting, 'You made a fool out of me. I won't stand for that.'

Bradley rushed at Ben, his big fists swinging. Ben ducked and caught Bradley on the jaw with an uppercut that sent him reeling back. 'Don't try it again,' Ben said. 'Keep a civil tongue in your head from now on. Don't forget that I'm giving the orders, and I'll keep on giving them as long as the Indians have got us penned up here.'

Bradley had recovered his balance, but he acted as if he hadn't heard a word Ben said. He picked up a rock as big as his fist and brought his arm back to throw it at Ben, still cursing with the fluency of a mule skinner. Wheeler leaped toward him, grabbed his right arm and twisted it until he dropped the rock.

Wheeler threw his left arm around Bradley's neck and pressed against his windpipe, all the time keeping Bradley's right arm back of his shoulder. As big and strong as the boy was, he was helpless in the preacher's grasp.

Wheeler eased the pressure on Bradley's

throat and asked, 'You ready to listen to reason?'

Bradley grunted something, and Wheeler said, 'All right, listen carefully. You and Melissa came here with me, but I am not responsible for your conduct. You and you alone are responsible. Either saddle up and ride on down the trail, or make up your mind to do what you're supposed to do. It's a clear choice.'

Wheeler released his grip on Bradley and stepped back. Bradley rubbed his throat, looked at the river, and brought his gaze back to Ben. 'All right, I'll do what I'm supposed to, but I think you're the fool. I haven't seen hide nor hair of any Injuns since we got here. I figure you're all a bunch of cowards afraid of shadows. After while I'm going to the river and see if there's any. If there ain't, Melissa and me are going on.'

'You won't do anything of the sort,' Ben said. 'You wouldn't accomplish anything except get yourself killed.'

'And you certainly won't take Melissa,' Wheeler added.

'Help water and feed the horses,' Ben said, and walked toward the house. He stopped to ask Bucky, 'Have you seen anything to make you think any of 'em are there?'

'No,' Bucky said. 'I think they've pulled out.'

'Well, we've got to act like they're still there,'

73

Ben said. 'Even if they did pull out, they may come back.'

Ben went inside to find Justin Miles sitting in a chair, awake and fully conscious. He said, 'Cherry tells me you saved my life. I don't remember nothing about what happened except that I was trying to get away from the Injuns.' He put a hand to his forehead and groaned. 'I've got one hell of a headache. I don't seem to remember anything real good.'

'I kept the Ute who was on the pinto from shooting you,' Ben said. 'You'll have to stay here till this blows over.'

'I didn't want to be beholden to you,' Miles said, 'but when a man saves your life...'

'You ain't beholden to me,' Ben said, 'but this is a good time to get something straight. Cherry and me are getting married. If you try to bust us up just to keep her for a cheap housekeeper, I'll break your god-damned neck.'

'I won't,' Miles said, and looked away, his face turning red.

Ben went on into the kitchen, thinking that Miles had no intention of keeping his word. Wheeler came in with Rick Bradley a few minutes later, saying, 'I'll spell Bucky off so he can have his supper.'

'Good,' Ben said. 'I'll be out after while.'

Bradley looked around. Anger, always just under the surface with him, rose when he didn't see Melissa. His big body began to tremble as

74

he asked, 'Where's my wife?'

'She's asleep,' Maudie said. 'She's gonna stay asleep and you're not gonna bother her.'

For a few seconds there was no sound in the kitchen except the crackling of pine in the firebox and the faint hissing of steam from a pan that was on the stove.

'You understand me, boy?' Maudie demanded.

Watching him, Ben thought he had never seen anyone filled with as much hate as 'Rick Bradley. Probably Wheeler was right in saying Melissa was a balance wheel. His wild temper turned him into a mad man without Melissa to guide and soothe him, and Ben, thinking he was about to explode into another fit of violence, took a step toward him expecting to give him the beating that had been promised.

But suddenly Bradley nodded and said, 'I understand.'

'Then sit down and enjoy your supper.'

The meal was a good one, but Ben felt the atmosphere crackling with pent-up hostility. Cherry sat next to him, and once her hand touched his lap. He slipped a hand under the table and held hers for a time, telling himself that the Indian scare had brought about at least one good thing.

When they finished eating, Maudie said, 'Fetch Wheeler in. I'll dish up his supper.'

'Bucky, you and Wheeler will stand guard till midnight,' Ben said. 'Bradley and me will

75

relieve you and take it till morning.'

Bucky nodded agreement, but Bradley demanded, 'What's the matter with the old man here?'

'I ain't well,' Miles whined.

'I ain't, either,' Ben said, 'but come daylight, you'll do your share the same as the rest of us.'

Ben walked out of the house, told Wheeler to go in and get his supper, and then started across the yard toward the barn. The dusk light was very thin now so that the dark shadows loomed ominously ahead of him. He stopped, his gaze probing the near darkness around the barn and corral.

He heard running steps behind him and turned. Cherry flew into his arms. She whispered, 'It's been such a long day, Ben.'

He held her for a moment before he said, 'It sure has. Things have got a lot worse since morning.'

'It'll work out,' she said. 'I know it will. It's kind of like having a high fever. You've got to have it and whip it before you can get any better.'

'I guess that's right,' he agreed, 'only we've got a long spell of fever ahead of us.'

He kissed her and sent her back into the house, then went on toward the corral. Bradley might be right in saying they were afraid of shadows, but you had to operate on the basis that the danger was real.

He could only be sure of one thing. A

situation like this was bound to bring out the best in a man like David Wheeler and the worst in Rick Bradley and Justin Miles. And he, Ben Holt, by virtue of his position, had to make use of everyone, good, bad, and indifferent.

CHAPTER NINE

As Cherry walked back to the house, she felt reassured. Ben's kiss and the brief moment he had held her in his arms did that for her. She would feel even better after she became Mrs Ben Holt. Wheeler was a preacher. There was no reason why he couldn't marry them tonight. Or tomorrow at least. She didn't want to wait, now that she had made up her mind.

She heard Ben's pounding steps behind her just as she reached the front door. Wheeler came through it, calling worriedly, 'Anything wrong?'

'Somebody's coming up the river,' Ben said. 'Fast. I don't know what it means.'

Wheeler stepped off the porch to stand beside Ben. He said, 'Yeah, he's moving, all right.'

'Grab my Henry rifle there by the door,' Ben said. 'I've got the Winchester. Get Bucky and Maudie out here. Tell 'em to fetch their rifles. Sounds like only one man, but there might be others behind him.'

77

Cherry stood frozen. She heard Wheeler call, 'Bucky! Maudie! Ben wants you out here. Bring your guns.'

Cherry heard Maudie and Bucky running out of the kitchen. The paralysis of fear left her as she turned to the door. There must be another gun somewhere, but she saw Rick Bradley jump out of his chair and run past her, shouting, 'Gimme your Winchester, Holt. I'll chase 'em across the river for you.' She watched her father get up from his chair and sit down again, his face turning gray.

The rider was very close now. Ben shouted, 'Who is it? Sing out.' No answer. Ben fired twice just as Maudie grabbed her Sharps from where it leaned against the wall and charged through the door, sending Cherry spinning to one side and Bucky to the other. She met Wheeler head on and spilled him on his back.

The rider was past the house now, the pound of hoofs fading. Cherry heard the bellow of Maudie's Sharps as Wheeler struggled to his feet. Ben asked, 'You couldn't see him, Maudie. What were you shooting at?'

'I heard him,' Maudie shouted. 'I was shooting at the sound...'

She stopped as if realizing she had done something that was completely stupid. Wheeler said in a tone of calm, controlled anger, 'You never want to get in front of Mrs Kregg when she's going somewhere in a hurry, Ben.'

'Yeah, Maudie,' Bucky said. 'You knocked me pizzle-end up on one side and Cherry on the other.'

'I'm sure glad I wasn't in front of her,' Rick Bradley said. 'When she went by me, it sounded like a herd of buffaloes had charged past.'

Maudie stood in the finger of lamplight that fell through the doorway. She was breathing hard, her face so red it was almost purple. Cherry thought she was going to have a stroke. Maudie was completely wrong and she knew it, Cherry thought, a situation she couldn't handle because she seldom did anything she couldn't defend.

Even now Maudie would not admit she was wrong. She said, 'Come back and finish your supper, Mr Wheeler. You didn't even get started on it.'

'What happened?' Justin Miles asked as Maudie lumbered past him on her way to the kitchen.

'Nothing, you old goat,' Maudie snapped. 'Nothing at all.'

Miles appeared in the doorway, snickering. 'First time in the two years I've lived on the river that I ever seen anybody get the best of that old war horse.'

Bucky wheeled on him. 'You've got a lot of gall...'

'All right, Bucky.' Ben laid a hand on his arm. 'We know he has.'

79

Miles grunted something and returned to his chair. Cherry asked, 'Who do you think he was and why was he riding like that?'

'I don't know,' Ben said. 'I couldn't see anything as long as he was against the willows, but when he rode past the ford, I made out a dark shape and that was all. That was when I fired. I didn't figure to hit him, but I thought I might scare him a little.'

'He rode like he was scared already,' Wheeler said. 'If he wasn't, Mrs Kregg's shot must have scared him clean over Gore Pass.'

'He was a white man, wasn't he?' Cherry asked.

'I figure he was,' Ben said, 'but don't ask me why he didn't answer when I hollered. He acted like he was as scared of us as he was of the Utes.'

'That doesn't make sense,' Wheeler said.

'Not much,' Ben admitted.

Cherry laid a hand on Wheeler's arm. 'You'd better go in and finish your supper or Maudie will be out here after you.'

'I wouldn't want that to happen,' Wheeler said, and went into the house.

'I wish I'd had a gun,' Rick Bradley said. 'I'd have got that bird for you and then you'd have known who he was.' He followed Wheeler into the house.

'He's not real. He can't be,' Ben said.

'Melissa is,' Cherry said. 'I feel sorry for her.'

She noticed that Ben had moved out of the
80

lamplight and both he and Bucky were standing motionless as if listening. Cherry whispered, 'What is it?'

'I keep wondering if the Utes were on his tail,' Ben said. 'A man don't ride like that very long, but if the Indians were right behind him, we'd have heard them before now.'

'He'd see our light quite a ways off,' Bucky said. 'Maybe he rode fast just going by here.'

'But why?' Cherry demanded. 'It just doesn't make any sense. If he was a white man, he'd want to stay with us. He'd know he would be safer here than trying to outrun the Indians.'

'There's one white man who wouldn't think that,' Ben said. 'That's Hank Long.'

'The trader?' Cherry said, surprised. 'He's dealt with the Indians for years. He'd be more likely to join them.'

'No, he's sold 'em some pretty shoddy stuff,' Ben said. 'They've been sore at him for a long time. He knows the settlers hate him for selling the Indians even poor guns, so he's caught in a squeeze.'

She put a hand on Ben's arm. 'I'd better go in and help Maudie with the dishes. I'll see you in the morning.'

'You sure will,' Ben said. 'Don't be afraid to sleep. They won't surprise us.'

She passed Wheeler on her way to the kitchen. He nodded at her and said, 'Good night, Miss Cherry.'

'Good night, Mr Wheeler,' she said, and

wished she had said something to him about marrying her and Ben, but knew she couldn't, that it was Ben's place to speak to the preacher. No man liked to be pushed, and she guessed Ben would think it was mighty queer that she had not encouraged him for two years, but now she couldn't wait to become his wife. Well, it didn't make much sense. All it proved was that she was like all other females, a glimpse of truth that did not please her.

When the dishes were put away, Maudie yawned and said, 'Glory be, this has been a day. I hope tomorrow ain't worse.'

Maudie ordered Justin Miles and Rick Bradley out of the front room, telling them their beds were waiting for them in the barn. She shut the door after them, picked up the bar that leaned against the wall, then put it down again.

'I ought to drop the bar across the door,' she said, 'but if there's trouble, the men will want in.' She grinned wryly. 'I guess I'd better let the men do the fightin'.'

Cherry picked up one of the lamps that was on the table and went into the bedroom, thinking that was about as close as Maudie would ever come to admitting she had been wrong in taking that blind shot at the rider. She closed the door softly so she would not wake Melissa, but the instant the door was shut, the girl sat up in bed and looked at Cherry.

'I'm sorry,' Cherry said. 'I didn't intend to

82

wake you.'

'You didn't,' Melissa said. 'The shooting woke me. I was just lying here and worrying about Rick. I didn't know what the shooting was about.'

Cherry told her as she set the lamp on the bureau and undressed. She glanced at Melissa, thinking how small and fragile she seemed. Her blond hair, clean and fluffy, fell down her back in a golden mass. She was wearing one of Ben's shirts for a nightgown which was far too big for her and made her look even smaller than she was. She didn't weigh over ninety pounds, and now that she'd had her bath she was, in Cherry's eyes, a very feminine and attractive girl.

Cherry slipped her nightgown on and sat down on the edge of the bed. 'You're a sweet and loyal wife, Melissa,' she said, 'but you're going to have to make Rick grow up into a man. He's not one now, you know, though he's big enough and strong enough to be one.'

Melissa nodded and began to cry. She wiped her eyes with her sleeve and swallowed. 'I know, but you see, it's my fault he's here. He has an awful temper, but he controls it when he's with me. He can't do things very well, so he brags to make folks think he's capable of doing anything. If he had stayed home and kept on working in his father's store, he would have grown up, but I got him to run away with me.'

Cherry put an arm around Melissa and

hugged her, feeling as motherly and protective as Maudie had that afternoon when she was giving Melissa a bath.

'Tell me about it,' Cherry said.

For a minute or two Melissa remained motionless, her head on Cherry's shoulder, then she pulled away so she could look at the other girl.

'I guess to someone like you who has a father who doesn't beat you and a friend like Mrs Kregg and a man like Mr Holt who loves you, it's hard to understand about me. You see, I never knew people could be kind until I met Mr Wheeler and then got here and met you folks.'

She brought her knees up under her chin and rocked back and forth for a moment, then she went on, 'You know how my mother beat me. I guess she had reason to part of the time because I wasn't always polite to her, but mostly it was because Pa drinks too much. He'd come home and beat Ma, and she'd get back at me. Well, I got so I just couldn't stand it any longer. I got Rick interested in me and talked him into running away. I guess if I went home now Ma would kill me, and Rick, he can't ever go back.'

She stopped talking, her eyes on the wall as if looking back at the misery-filled years she had spent at home. Cherry asked, 'Why can't Rick go back?'

'Oh.' She glanced at Cherry, startled. 'Why, when we decided what we were going to do, we

84

knew we had to have some money and neither one of us had a dollar, so Rick stole his father's savings. It was hidden in the cellar. It wasn't much, about eight hundred dollars, but it was all Mr Bradley had. If he ever got hold of Rick he'd send him to prison.'

Cherry nodded, wanting Melissa to know she understood. She thought about her own home which had become unbearable, and yet it had never been as bad as Melissa's. She didn't doubt the girl's story, not after having seen the scars on her back.

'We still have almost all the money,' Melissa went on. 'That's what Rick wants to buy a ranch with, but I don't know. Maybe it would be better if we worked for awhile. I'm strong and I've worked hard ever since I was little. If Rick will just stop bragging and quit getting mad at folks, he could keep a job.'

'There's quite a few people who live on down the river,' Cherry said. 'Let me sleep on it. Maybe I can think of somebody who would give you work.'

Cherry blew out the lamp and slipped into bed beside Melissa. The other girl was asleep in a minute or two, but Cherry lay awake a long time. She doubted that Rick Bradley would ever grow up, and she could not see anything but trouble ahead for Melissa. She wished she could do something for the girl, but all she could think of was to tell her to go back home, but she knew Melissa would not do that.

Maybe it would be wrong, anyhow. How was she, Cherry Miles, to know for sure? And how was she to know for sure that it was wrong to ask Ben to have Wheeler marry them tomorrow?

She could not bear the thought of losing Ben, and she was afraid she would if they waited. She didn't know why, but the fear was there and lingered in her mind in spite of anything she could do. Suddenly the wonderful and surprising peace that had been in her earlier this evening was no longer there.

CHAPTER TEN

The guard duty that lasted until midnight was almost more than Bucky Kregg could bear. The darkness was filled with strange sounds; the barn and corral were alive with shadows, any one of which might be an Indian. He had dreamed of situations like this in which he would save Maudie's and Ben's life, and later Ben would pat him on the back and tell him he was a stout fellow, and Maudie would say she had known all the time that he was filled with man stuff.

Now he had no idea why he ever had such dreams. If he failed to beat off an attack, or give a warning and the Utes stole the horses, he could never look Maudie or Ben in the face again. But he might not have to. He might get killed. Once or twice, when he let his thoughts run that way, he discovered tears running down his cheeks. He gritted his teeth and wiped a sleeve across his eyes.

The only thing that saved him was David Wheeler appearing out of the darkness once in a while and asking if everything was all right. Wheeler was a good man, just about as good a man as Ben. He probably didn't know what it was to be afraid and Bucky didn't aim to let him know how he felt, so he always sang out in a strong voice that everything was all right.

Later, and it seemed a long time later, Ben and Rick Bradley came out of the barn, Ben telling Bradley not to shoot at anything until he was sure it was an Indian. Bucky gave his Winchester to Bradley and wished he didn't have to. Bradley was the jumpy kind. Bucky didn't believe he was half as brave as he claimed to be. He might even be a little crazy.

'All quiet?' Ben asked.

'Sure is,' Bucky answered.

'Good,' Ben said. 'Now you go and catch yourself a nap.'

Bucky didn't realize he was cold until he was inside the barn where it was warm. He found a blanket on the hay and pulled it over him. Presently Wheeler came in and lay down. For a time Bucky was vaguely aware of the horses kicking against the sides of their stalls and of Justin Miles's snoring. Then Ben was shaking

87

him and saying, 'Maudie just hollered breakfast. Better come or she'll be mad.'

Ben shook Miles awake. He said, 'You've slept all night, Justin. I guess you're over your headache by now, so you'll take a whack at guard duty today.'

Miles blinked owlishly. He said, 'Well now, Holt, I'd like to, but my head...'

Ben stooped and grabbed Miles by a shoulder and dragged him outside. Miles sputtered, 'Hold on now. Take it easy. I said I'd like to...'

Bucky didn't hear the rest of what Miles had to say. He watched Ben drag Miles across the yard to the horse trough and jam his face into the cold water. Ben yanked Miles back and let him sputter as he fought for breath, then rammed his head back into the water. This time when he let Miles up, he shoved his Winchester at Miles who took it, still sputtering and gasping as he wiped his face with the sleeve of his free arm.

'You're a hard man,' Miles managed to say. 'If I was a little younger, I'd whip you till...'

'You bet I'm a hard man,' Ben said in cold fury. 'If you were a little younger, you wouldn't do no different than you're doing right now. I'll tell you something else,' he tapped Miles's chest with a forefinger, 'if the Utes are gonna make a try for our horses, this is about the time of day they'll do it. If you go to sleep or wander off so you can't see 'em when they leave the river, I'll kick you bow-legged.'

Ben wheeled and strode toward the house. Miles shambled toward the corral, the rifle in his right hand. He swiped his left arm across his face again and disappeared around the barn. Bucky washed at the horse trough as Wheeler and Bradley walked toward him. They had seen what had happened, and Bradley was scowling. When they reached the trough, Bradley said, 'Who does this Holt think he is, kicking us around like he owns us?'

'He's the man who'll keep us alive if anyone does,' Wheeler said. 'We'll be fighting for our lives before this is over. Don't you forget it the next time he asks you to do something.'

Bradley sulked, but he didn't talk back. Bucky had a notion that Wheeler had had about all of Rick Bradley he could stomach. He grinned as he followed Ben into the house. Before this was over, David Wheeler might teach Bradley a thing or two.

Bucky had not realized how hungry he was until he went into the house and smelled coffee, flapjacks, and frying bacon. Maudie said cheerfully, 'Sit down, men, and eat hearty or you'll hurt the cooks' feelings.'

Cherry stood at the stove turning the flapjacks and Melissa was setting a platter of them on the table. Bucky stared at Melissa, wide-eyed. Her dress was washed and ironed, she was clean, her cheeks were a healthy pink, and her gold-blond hair was tied at the back of her head with a pink ribbon.

'Look who's all prettied up,' Ben said.

Wheeler nodded approvingly. 'Melissa, you remind me of a caterpillar that went into hiding and came out a beautiful butterfly.'

Melissa tried to smile, but the corners of her mouth started to quiver, so she glanced away. Bucky said admiringly, 'You sure are pretty, Melissa.' He didn't believe she was old enough to be married. She couldn't be much older than he was.

Melissa glanced covertly at her husband to see if he approved of the way she looked, but he was already helping himself liberally to the flapjacks and didn't act as if he knew she was in the room. Melissa whirled and went back to the stove to stand beside Cherry.

'Stop it, all of you,' Maudie said crossly. 'You're just making Melissa nervous.'

'It's all right, Mrs Kregg,' Melissa said. 'It's nice to know that ... that someone thinks you're pretty.'

Bradley poured syrup on his flapjacks and took a big bite. He didn't even know what Melissa was talking about, Bucky thought. He hadn't liked Rick Bradley from the time he'd ridden in with Melissa and Wheeler, but now Bucky hated him.

When they finished eating, Maudie said, 'Ben, you're running this show and I ain't fixing to tell you how to do it, but I've got an idea. Want to hear it?'

Ben grinned. 'I may be running the show, but I ain't above listening to ideas.'

'Well, you know Bucky was digging our potatoes yesterday when we decided we'd better get over here. We only brought a few. Most of 'em are just setting there on top of the ground. If the sun gets through the clouds today, it won't do them potatoes no good.'

'I guess we oughtta take care of 'em for you,' Ben said.

'What I was thinking was that maybe Bucky could hitch up the wagon and him and one other man, maybe Mr Wheeler 'cause if we have trouble you oughtta be on hand to handle it, could go fetch back another sack of spuds and put the rest in the root cellar. They can bring a ham that's in the kitchen. Bucky had better throw some cabbage and turnips into the wagon, too.'

'Good idea.' Ben nodded at Wheeler. 'Want to try it, Dave?'

'Sure,' Wheeler said, 'unless you think splitting us up will make you too weak here.'

Bucky knew what he was trying to say, that Rick Bradley and Justin Miles were worth nothing and that left Ben alone. Bucky watched Ben as he thought about it and he sensed that Ben was more concerned about the situation than he let on. They needed the food, Bucky knew, and that was probably what decided Ben.

'Maudie's got her Sharps,' Ben said finally,

91

'and Cherry is a pretty good hand with a rifle. You go ahead. Maudie's right about trouble being here if we have any. More'n one Ute buck has tried to buy my black saddle horse, so the chances are this is the place they'll attack if they try it anywhere.'

Bucky rose. 'I'll harness up, Mr Wheeler. It won't take long.'

'I'll give you a hand,' Wheeler said.

Neither said much as they drove upstream. Bucky kept watching the willows along the river. The fact that he didn't see or hear anything that indicated the Indians were hiding there was little comfort. He knew the Utes too well. They could move like shadows so they could be right beside you and you wouldn't know they were there until they wanted you to know it.

They tied the team beside the barn. Even after they started sacking the potatoes and carrying the sacks to the wagon, Bucky found himself glancing at the river time after time. They kept their rifles beside them but there wasn't any protection out here in the middle of the garden.

The minutes passed, Bucky's heart hammering with great sledging beats. His chest pressed against his lungs so it became harder and harder for him to breathe. They finished sacking the potatoes, and carried the extra sacks into the root cellar, but the passing minutes did not make Bucky feel any easier. He knew they would have trouble before they got back to Ben's place. He did not have any idea why he knew it, but he was as certain as he was that the sun would go down in the evening.

Bucky did not mention this to Wheeler, but kept on working. They pulled enough turnips for several meals and tossed them into the wagon. They felt the cabbage heads and found three that were solid enough to eat and dropped them into the wagon. For just a few seconds Bucky doubted his hunch. He had never seen the valley more peaceful than at that moment. Nothing moved except the willow leaves shivering in the breeze that flowed down from the mountain, then he glanced at the house and his heart flipped up into his mouth. He gave a low, strangled cry that didn't sound like any noise he had ever made before in his life.

'What is it?' Wheeler asked.

He was about three steps from Bucky still feeling cabbage heads. Now he picked up the Henry rifle and straightened, his eyes on Bucky.

'There's a white man in the house,' Bucky said. 'I seen his face in the window for a little while, then it disappeared.'

'He's been watching us all the time,' Wheeler said. 'He hasn't hurt us, so he probably doesn't intend to, but Mrs Kregg would be mad if we went off and left him in there.'

'She sure would,' Bucky said hoarsely.

'Anyhow, she wanted that ham she told us to get.'

Wheeler put his hand to the small of his back as if it hurt. He said, 'You drive the wagon to the back door. He won't think anything about it if you stop close to the root cellar. I'll go across the potato patch and pretend I'm looking for some we missed. That'll put me close to the front door. I'll make a run for it and we'll have him bottled up, but we'd better be careful we don't shoot each other.'

Bucky nodded, not liking it but at the moment unable to think of a better plan. He turned with feigned carelessness toward the wagon, but he took only one step when the man in the house yelled, 'Look out.' Bucky instinctively dropped flat into the dirt and scrambled around so he faced the river.

One moment the valley had been perfectly quiet, the next a dozen or more Utes burst out of the willows, filling the air with their hideous yells as they whipped their horses into a run and drove straight toward the house in a headlong charge.

Bucky started shooting the instant he saw the Indians. The man in the house cut loose, and a few seconds later Wheeler began firing. One brave tumbled off his horse as if he had run into a tight wire. Two horses stumbled and fell, their riders sliding off safely before their mounts went down.

The lead Indian was riding a pinto. He gave

94

a sweeping signal with his right hand and the entire bunch that was still mounted whirled and raced back into the willows, disappearing almost as fast as they had come into view.

Three Utes were on foot. Two of them fired, one bullet kicking up dust within a foot of Bucky's head. The third brave had been hurt enough by his fall to slow him up and make him limp. The other two raced past him toward the willows. Bucky emptied his Winchester, trying to bring down the slow Indian, but he succeeded in reaching the willows a few steps behind the others. Now that it was too late, Bucky realized he had been firing too rapidly and probably had not hit any of them.

Bucky rose and dropped flat as half a dozen shots crackled from the willows, one bullet snapping past his head so close that he spilled flat on the ground without thinking, then lay there for a moment thankful he was still alive.

He crawled toward the back door of the house, wondering what had happened to Wheeler. The preacher wasn't in sight, but Bucky knew he couldn't stand up and look, not after escaping death by an inch or so as he had a few seconds before. As long as he wormed his way along the ground, the Indians didn't have much of a target.

When Bucky reached the rear of the house he rose and lunged through the back door. There, in the kitchen a few feet in front of him, he saw David Wheeler standing motionless, the muzzle of his rifle jammed into the back of a bearded man Bucky recognized at once.

'He's Hank Long,' Bucky said. 'He's the one who's got the trading post down the river from Hayden.'

'Did have,' Long said angrily. 'The bastards burned me out.'

Long was a small man with a wiry beard that seemed to friz out all over his face except from his eyes and nose. He wore dirty buckskin and moccasins, and he stank of stale sweat and horse manure. To Bucky he was a completely disagreeable man.

'Get the ham,' Wheeler said. 'We'd better clear out of here as fast as we can. I don't savvy this, though. They could have ridden us down if they'd kept coming.'

'They're after me,' Long said. 'They figured you two would run and they'd just have one man to root out of the house.'

'That was you who rode past last night, wasn't it?' Bucky asked.

'Yeah, it was me and I got shot at,' Long said. 'Now will you fellers get a move on. They might decide to tackle the house.'

Bucky found the ham in the pantry. He ran after the other two who had reached the wagon. He expected to hear shots again every time he took a step and maybe feel the numbing impact of a slug slamming into his back, but there was no more shooting.

Long led his horse out of the barn. Wheeler

said, 'Tie him behind the wagon. I've got a hunch Ben Holt will want to ask you some questions.'

'Naw, I'm riding over Gore Pass,' Long said. 'I should have done it last night,'

'The Indians will kill you before you've gone a hundred yards,' Wheeler said. 'Here, I'll ride your horse. That'll be better than tying him behind the wagon. Get up into the seat with Bucky.'

Long scratched a bearded cheek, his gaze whipping from Wheeler to Bucky and back to Wheeler. He was jumpy enough to panic and do something crazy, Bucky thought. He called, 'Watch him, Mr Wheeler.'

'I'm watching him,' Wheeler said. 'If he does the wrong thing, he'll get a dose of lead poisoning. From what I've heard about him, he's long overdue.'

'He is,' Bucky said.

'Now climb into that wagon,' Wheeler said.

This was the first time he had seen Wheeler angry and for a moment Bucky thought he would start cursing the man. But he didn't. He jammed the muzzle of the rifle into Long's belly, his mouth tightening into a thin, down-curving line.

Long started to step up to the seat, then stopped. He said, 'You don't know what you're doing, mister. Holt and Maudie Kregg and Justin Miles will put a rope on my neck the minute you turn me over to 'em.'

'They won't do anything of the kind,' Wheeler said. 'I give you my word.'

Long hesitated, staring at Wheeler as if he wanted to believe him, then he climbed up and sat down beside Bucky. Bucky spoke to the team as Wheeler mounted Long's horse, then a new thought sent terror surging through him again.

He had thought the Utes were letting them go, but now he knew better. Halfway between Maudie's and Ben's houses the river made a loop so that it came almost to the road at one point. If the Utes had ridden downstream and were hiding in the willows at that particular place, they'd open fire and they'd have three easy scalps.

'Hang on,' Bucky yelled at Long.

He lashed the horses into a run with the ends of the lines and pulled off the road into a hay field. The wagon bounced over the rough ground like a jack rabbit; it lurched and swung back and forth with the crazy violence that the end man feels in a game of crack the whip. Hank Long, his eyes bugging out of his head in fear, hung onto the seat with both hands. Bucky didn't look at him. All he could think of was getting back to Ben's place.

CHAPTER ELEVEN

Ben harnessed his team, hooked them up to his wagon, and pulled the load of hay around the corral to the unfinished stack on the opposite side from the gate. He began forking hay from the wagon to the stack, then stopped and wiped his forehead. He glanced at the sun that was moving upward into a clear sky and told himself the day would be a warm one, typical of the Indian summer days that he had enjoyed so much since he'd come to the Yampa.

The heavy clouds which had covered the peaks to the east yesterday were gone, and he did not feel the bite in the air which had made him think winter was at hand. Usually he would have been thankful for a warm day on the first of October, but today he wished the threatened storm had developed. As dry as it was, the Utes would have little trouble burning him out if they set their minds to it.

Well, he'd worry about that when it happened. Right now the problem was to keep from being surprised. He kept his eyes on the willows along the river as he worked, and told himself he shouldn't have let Wheeler and Bucky leave here. They'd be easy pickings for the Utes, and it would be difficult to defend the house while they were gone.

Justin Miles and Rick Bradley were talking

beside the corral gate. Ben had no idea what their conversation was about, but occasionally they glanced covertly at him. They reminded him of two disobedient children who were hatching some kind of plot against the teacher.

The truth was that neither Miles nor Bradley would be worth a plugged nickel if the Indians attacked the house. Miles was lazy and shiftless and would never assume any responsibility he could avoid. Bradley was a loud-voiced braggart who had to cover his deficiencies by his boasting. In a few days the Indian scare would be over with and he'd have Bradley off his back, but Justin Miles would still be here.

Ben began forking hay onto the stack again, a sullen anger building up in him. The thought of having Miles for a father-in-law was more than he could bear. He had no choice if he wanted to marry Cherry.

He jabbed his fork into the hay and straightened up, his thoughts turning to Wheeler and Bucky again. It would be hell on high, red wheels if the Indians murdered them. He would never forgive himself. No sense blaming Maudie. Sure, it had been her suggestion, but he had agreed to it, and as she had said, he was the one giving the orders.

On impulse he jumped off the wagon, picked up his rifle, and saddled his black gelding. He jammed the Winchester into the boot and led the horse around the corral to the wagon. He hesitated, looking upstream toward Maudie's place. The temptation to mount and ride over there was very strong, but he couldn't risk it. Logic still told him that if there was trouble it would be right here where the horses were, but he also knew that there was little relationship between logic and the actions of a band of Indians, particularly young braves.

Ordinarily Ben was not a man who had trouble making decisions, but he had trouble now. He was still standing beside his horse when the sound of rifle fire from up the river came to him and made his decision for him. As he swung into the saddle he had the weird feeling that he had known all the time it would turn out this way; that Wheeler and Bucky were the ones in danger and he should have followed his hunch and gone after them.

As Ben rounded the corral he saw that Rick Bradley was halfway to the house, but Miles had remained at the gate, his head cocked as if he wasn't sure what was happening.

'Unhook my team and put 'em in the barn, Justin,' Ben yelled as he rode past Miles.

When he thundered by the house, he glimpsed Maudie standing on the porch. He saw concern on her face and told himself that she'd go crazy if she lost Bucky. She was tough, almost brutal with the boy at times, but as far as she was concerned, the sun rose and set in him.

When he was close enough to Maudie's farm to see the house and barn and yard clearly, he

101

was shocked to discover that nothing was happening. He had expected to see the Indians milling around the place, maybe circling it on their horses, but he didn't see anyone. Nothing moved. He was sick with fear, certain that Bucky and Wheeler had been surprised and had been cut down in the first blast of rifle fire.

For a moment he was tempted to turn back, thinking that if the Utes had taken over the house and barn they'd let him come on in and dismount and then they'd cut him to pieces. His death would leave Cherry and the others almost defenseless and he couldn't risk that.

Again he was caught in a bog of indecision, but it lasted only a few seconds because he caught movement to his left. Turning his head, he saw Maudie's wagon bouncing crazily over her hay field. It was on the other side next to the base of the hill. The horses were running as hard as they could, Bucky was driving, a man sat beside him on the seat, and a third man was on a horse keeping pace behind the wagon.

Ben had no idea why Bucky was taking the wagon across the hay field, but it seemed crazy to him. Bucky must have panicked. The way he was driving he could ruin the horses, smash up Maudie's wagon, and kill himself and the man on the seat beside him.

Ben swung his black off the road and put him into a hard run, angling across the field, but he didn't catch up with the wagon until it was within one hundred yards of his house.

'Pull up,' Ben yelled at Bucky as he came alongside. 'No one's chasing you. Pull up.'

'Injuns,' Bucky yelled back. 'They damn near got us.'

Ben recognized Hank Long on the seat beside Bucky. Dave Wheeler must be on Long's horse, Ben thought. He yelled again, 'Pull up.' When he saw that Bucky wasn't trying to stop, he shouted, 'Pull up or I'll do it for you.'

Bucky sawed on the lines, slowing the team and stopping them a moment later. Ben looked at the heaving, sweating horses and shook his head at Bucky. He said, 'Justin almost killed his team yesterday, but the Utes were right behind him, so there was some sense to what he done. What excuse have you got?'

Bucky looked across the field toward the river, swallowed, opened his mouth to say something, then got red in the face and didn't say a word. Long said sharply, 'They was after us, Holt. They attacked the house a little bit ago with me in it. The Kregg boy and the other feller were in the spud patch. It's a wonder all of us ain't dead.'

Wheeler had stopped his mount beside Ben's black. He said gravely, 'Bucky did the right thing. He saw no reason to save the horses and risk our lives.'

Ben studied the preacher's face. Obviously he hadn't panicked. Maybe Bucky hadn't, either. 'All right, son,' Ben said. 'Tell me about it.'

Bucky moistened dry lips with the tip of his tongue. He said, 'They came charging out of the brush along the river. We didn't have no warning. We beat 'em off. I dunno whether we killed any of 'em, but we hit some of 'em all right. The trouble was we didn't know what they'd do next.'

The boy motioned toward the river. 'I figured they might be hiding where the brush gets close to the road. If they was, they'd knock us kicking afore we had a chance, so I pulled into the field, figuring we'd best keep as far from the river as we could.'

'You used your noggin,' Ben said. 'All right, go ahead. Just take it easy. When we get home, you'll have to look after your horses.'

'I will,' Bucky said.

The wagon moved on, slowly now, and Ben dropped back to ride beside Wheeler. He asked, 'How'd Long get into this?'

'He was hiding in the house,' Wheeler said. 'He claims the Indians are after him. They charged us, figuring that Bucky and I would run, I guess. When we stayed and fought, they turned around and lit out for the brush again. Looked like they didn't have the stomach to fight three men.'

'He knew they were after him last night,' Ben said, 'or he wouldn't have been riding the way he was.'

'I guess he did.' Wheeler hesitated, then he

said bluntly, 'You were too hard on the boy, Ben. He's got plenty of sand in his craw. He lay there in the garden and fired away like an old Indian fighter. I have a hunch he was the only one of us who hit any of them. I'll admit I was scared. When you see a dozen of them all painted up and riding right at you it's something to be scared about.'

'You're absolutely right and I'd have been scared, too.' Ben smiled, realizing that Wheeler was reprimanding him in his quiet way. 'It's like this, Dave. Out here we figure any man or boy has got sand in his craw. If he don't, he won't stay. He shouldn't have come in the first place. Rick Bradley's that kind. He talks big, but he's a coward and I'm purty sure that when the blue chip is down, he'll do something dangerous and stupid.'

'I still don't savvy why you scolded Bucky,' Wheeler said.

'You run horses the way he was doing only when you have to,' Ben said. 'Bucky should have figured out from the way the Utes pulled back that they weren't likely to chase the three of you.'

Wheeler shook his head. 'I don't see how he could have.'

'It's like Long said. They're after him, not you and Bucky. I don't know just what this bunch has got against Long, but it looks like it's more'n selling 'em poor rifles and faulty ammunition. I'll get it out of him if I have to beat him to death.'

'They were after Miles yesterday,' Wheeler reminded him.

'Sure they were,' Ben agreed, 'but you see, Justin was never friendly to 'em. He wouldn't feed 'em when they were hungry. He'd run 'em off with a shotgun, so when they had a chance to settle some scores, he was one they wanted to settle with. Indians have good memories.' He thought about it a moment, then added, 'I don't think they're going to worry much about Justin. I mean, not feeding 'em wasn't a real big thing and they might forget it, but it looks to me that they ain't gonna forget Long.'

'Then he's done something that was real bad by their standards,' Wheeler said.

Ben nodded. 'And their standards ain't always like ours. The way you look at it, Nathan Meeker was doing good for 'em, but to them he was poison mean.'

'So he's dead,' Wheeler said. 'I came here to help him, but I was too late.'

'You couldn't have helped him if you'd come six months ago,' Ben said. 'Nobody could have helped him. He wouldn't let them.'

Wheeler nodded as if he understood what Ben meant. He seemed to be thinking about something that was bothering him. Then he said, 'You're trying to tell me that this bunch of young braves won't hurt the rest of us. All they want is Long?'

'That's about the size of it,' Ben said, 'except

that I wouldn't say they won't hurt us. I don't think they really care about the rest of us one way or the other, but the point is we've got Long and that puts all of us in the fire unless we turn him loose, which we won't do.'

'Then I made a mistake,' Wheeler said. 'I made him come. He was going to take out for Gore Pass. He claimed that you and Mrs Kregg and Miles would hang him.'

'He deserves it and he knows it,' Ben said, 'but he never in the world would have got to Middle Park. They'd have killed him before he was halfway over Gore Pass. As much as I hate him, I wouldn't want him or any white man to be tortured the way they'd have tortured him.'

They rode in silence then, Wheeler's somber expression indicating that he still condemned himself for forcing Long to come back with them.

Ben didn't pay any attention to Wheeler. He had expected the Indians to make a try for the horses, but they hadn't. Now it was different. They had a double reason to attack. He asked himself if the horses plus Long's presence would be enough to trigger a serious assault. He would know, he thought, once he found out what Long had done to make them hate him so much.

CHAPTER TWELVE

Maudie and Cherry were waiting in front of the house, Maudie's broad face showing her concern. Justin Miles walked toward them from the corral, and Melissa and Rick Bradley stood in the doorway, Rick's arm around his wife's tiny waist, both of them looking uneasy as if poised for flight.

Maudie moved toward the wagon even before Bucky pulled up, shouting, 'What happened, Bucky? What happened?' Then she recognized Hank Long and stood motionless, staring at him as she might have stared at a rattlesnake that had suddenly appeared in the path in front of her.

'We took care of the spuds,' Bucky said, 'and we've got some turnips and cabbage in the wagon. We got the ham, too. It was kind of scary there for a minute...'

The boy stopped, seeing that Maudie wasn't listening. Now, as Ben and Wheeler dismounted, she exploded, cursing Long until she ran out of breath. She stopped, then whirled to face Ben who was walking toward her leading his black.

'You must have a rope somewhere around this place, Ben,' Maudie bellowed. 'Where is it?'

'Well now,' Ben said softly, 'just what would

you do with a rope if you had it?'

She glared at Ben, her face turning red and gradually darkening until it was almost purple. 'You know what I'd do with it. I'd hang this bastard. That's what I'd do.'

'I just now remember, Maudie,' Ben said. 'I don't have a rope on the place.'

'I do,' Justin Miles called. 'It's in the wagon.'

'Get it,' Maudie shouted. 'I'll tie the knot myself. We'll take him down there to the river. That cottonwood next to the ford has a limb that'll hold him.'

Long sat hunched forward on the wagon seat beside Bucky as if he were frozen, his tiny, red-flecked eyes whipping from Maudie to Ben and back to Maudie. Now he cried shrilly, 'Wheeler, you said there wouldn't be no hanging if I came with you.'

'There won't,' Wheeler said as if disgusted by this whole performance. 'Miles, don't get that rope. I'm surprised at you, Mrs Kregg. You're acting as blood-thirsty as the savages we fought a few minutes ago.'

'Stay out of this, preacher,' Maudie bellowed. 'You don't know what Long's done. Your friend Meeker and the rest of 'em at the agency would be alive right now if Long...'

'All right, Maudie,' Ben said. 'You've had your cussing exercise for the morning. Now go tend to your housework the way you're supposed to and leave the outside business to men.' He motioned for Long to get down.

'Come on, Hank. You'n me have some talking to do.'

Long stepped down, his rifle held on the ready. He said, 'You ain't gonna put no rope on my neck. I never killed a woman, but I will if you try to hang me.'

Justin Miles had stopped halfway across the yard to his wagon. Now he started toward it again. Wheeler covered him with his rifle as he called angrily, 'Miles, if you get that rope, I'll kill you.'

Miles stopped again. He turned and stared at Wheeler as if not certain he had heard right.

Maudie gasped. She said, 'I never seen the beat of it. Have you gone crazy, preacher, talking about killing a man who don't want nothing except to see justice done?'

'I promised Long there would be no hanging,' Wheeler said. 'I'll keep that promise. Don't make any mistake about it.'

'Don't you know you've got a thief, a cheat and a murderer who deserves hanging?' Maudie demanded. 'Meeker done his best to get Long to quit trading guns to the Indians, but he kept right on doing it. Now we've got him . . .'

'The fun's over,' Ben said. 'Get back to your job of cooking our dinner before I run out of patience and put you across my knee and whale your fat behind.'

'You put me across your knee?' Maudie was outraged by the thought. 'Ben Holt, you never

110

seen the day you could come close to doing that. You try it and I'll pull your arms out of their sockets. I'll knock you down into the dirt and I'll jump on you.'

Ben leaned his rifle against the wagon. 'All right, Maudie, why don't you try it?'

Nobody had called Maudie's bluff in the two years she had lived on the Yampa. She glared at Ben, blinking. She opened her mouth and closed it. She wiped a hand across her face and swallowed, then turned on her heel, grunting, 'Come on, Cherry. Let's start dinner.'

Bradley and Melissa stepped out of the doorway to let Maudie sail through, Cherry a step behind her. Wheeler said, as if he couldn't believe it, 'They'd have hanged him if we'd let them. What's wrong with people, Ben? It would have been murder.'

'That's why we had to stop it,' Ben said, 'but let's not forget that Maudie was right about Long being a thief, a cheat, and a murderer. Meeker did try to get Long to quit trading guns to the Utes, but as agent he didn't have any real power off the reservation.'

'But hanging a man is lynching,' Wheeler protested. 'We could all be arrested for murder.'

'That's right.' Ben handed the reins to Wheeler. 'Unsaddle my horse and take care of Long's. Bucky, you rub your team down good.' He jerked his head at Long. 'Come on.'

Ben strode toward the corral, Long

111

following, his wary gaze on Justin Miles who was still standing where he had stopped when Wheeler had told him he'd kill him if he brought the rope.

When Ben reached Miles, he said, 'Justin, you don't hate Long any more than I do, but you're not going to lay a hand on him while he's here. If you do, the fact that you're Cherry's father won't help you. I'll beat you half to death. You savvy?'

'You bet I savvy,' Miles said bitterly. 'All you need to beat me up is an excuse. Well, I'm not giving it to you if I can help it.'

Miles strode toward the house, his face hard set. He stopped to talk to Bradley and Melissa, then the three of them walked around the house. Ben went on to the wagon load of hay on the opposite side of the corral, motioning for Long to follow him. As he climbed up on the hay, he wondered what kind of shenanigan Miles was trying to work on the young couple.

Long remained on the ground, his grizzly face questioning Ben as he looked up at him. 'Get up here,' Ben ordered. 'We can talk while I'm forking this hay off the wagon. Leave your rifle on the ground. You won't need it up here.'

Long hesitated, glanced at the brush along the river as if expecting the Indians to come after him again, then he shrugged, leaned his Winchester against the front of the wagon, and climbed up.

'Gimme a fork and I'll help,' Long said. 'Or I

112

can get over there on the stack and top it out for you. I ain't been a trader all my life. I used to build a purty fair haystack when I was farming.'

Ben shook his head. 'No, I want to talk and I want you to keep your mind on your talking. I'll give you one warning, Hank. Don't lie to me. I'll know it if you are, and I'll make you wish you'd never lied to anybody in your life.'

'I wouldn't lie to you, Ben,' Long said plaintively. 'I know you too well. You'd be mean ornery.'

'You're right,' Ben said. 'Now then, you made a purty fair chunk of *dinero* out of your trading post, didn't you?'

Long nodded. 'I done good. I was there better'n three years and I cleared 'bout five thousand. I used to farm on the South Platte, but the Panic of '73 cleaned me out. We moved to Denver and damn near starved till I came to the Yampa. I've sent my wife all the money I could spare and she's saved all of it. She got a job and didn't need my money to live on. Now I'm going to Denver to live with her. It's time we enjoyed ourselves a little.'

'Got any children?'

'No. Good thing, I reckon, the way it's been with us. You and the rest have been calling me some purty ugly names. Thief. Cheat. Murderer. Well sir, I've risked my life with them red devils. If me and my wife hadn't almost starved to death, I never would have

113

come here in the first place. If you'd gone through what I had, maybe you'd be all the things you claim I am.'

'I doubt it,' Ben said. 'How'd you hear 'bout the Indian trouble?'

'Rankin and Gordon and a couple of soldiers stopped at the Post Monday night. I knew the Utes would be along, so I pulled out as soon as Rankin and the others left. I saddled that chestnut I'm riding and hid in a ravine. The red devils showed up just like I knew they would and burned every building I had.'

'That was Tuesday morning?'

'That's right,' Long said. 'Early. They pulled out before daylight, but I was close enough to recognize some of 'em in the light of the fire. They'd have cut me up good if they'd caught me, so I waited till they were back across the river.'

'Who was leading 'em?'

'Nosho,' Long answered. 'He's so little he looks like a kid, but he's twenty. Maybe more. He rides a pinto. Fastest horse they've got.'

He was probably the brave who had led the attack on Justin Miles, Ben thought. It would have meant hard riding, but Nosho's band could have arrived here by cutting across Twenty Mile Park if they had left Long's trading post before daylight. The chances were they guessed Long would head for Gore Pass and they expected to cut him off somewhere near its western base.

'Why didn't you stop at Hayden or Steamboat Springs?' Ben asked. 'You knew the Utes would have enough men strung out between here and your post to pick up your trail.'

Long turned sullen. 'I tried to stop at Hayden, but they was gonna hang me just like the Kregg woman and Miles wanted to, only there was a bunch of 'em and nobody like Wheeler made 'em behave. I was lucky to get away alive.'

'You rode hard when you went past here, figuring we'd hang you, too,' Ben said.

'Sure I did,' Long snarled. 'Somebody shot at me, so I knowed damn well I couldn't stop. I seen there wasn't no light in Mrs Kregg's house. I holed up there 'cause me'n my horse was about done up. I aimed to go on after dark, but Nosho or some of his bunch must have been along here and figured out where I was when they didn't hear my horse no more.'

It was more likely he had showed himself at a window, Ben thought, and the Indians, watching from the brush, had seen him. He pitched several forkfuls of hay to the stack, considered what Long had said, then he stopped and remarked, 'It was a good thing for you that Wheeler and Bucky were there this morning.'

'Yeah, I guess so,' Long admitted, 'but I wanted to go on to Middle Park, only Wheeler made me come here. It wasn't my idea to move

115

in with you.'

'I don't want you here any more than you want to be here,' Ben said, 'but you're a white man, so we'll let you stay till it's safe to go on.'

'Thanks.' Long's mouth curled down at the corners. 'Thanks a whole damn lot. I'm gonna enjoy the company of Maudie Kregg and Justin Miles.'

Ben leaned on the handle of the pitchfork. He said, 'Why are Nosho and his bucks so determined to get you?'

'You know without me telling you,' Long said, turning sullen again. 'I got a good buy on guns. I traded 'em for ponies and buckskin which I sold in Rawlins at a good profit, on account of I got the guns dirt cheap. They was old and a little rusty, and it made the Utes sore when they saw 'em, but they took 'em 'cause they couldn't do no better.'

'You're lying, Hank,' Ben said. 'I told you I'd know.'

'No, by God, I ain't lying,' Long shouted. 'You've heard it same as everybody else on the river.'

'I've heard it and it's true as far as it goes,' Ben said. 'That's where the lie is. You've done something else.'

Long glared at Ben. 'No. I didn't do nothing else.'

Ben took one long, quick step toward Long, swinging the tines of the fork upward from the hay so that the sharp points came straight at the soft part of the man's belly. Long let out a

116

scared yip and backed up, but he lost his footing in the hay and sprawled on his back. Ben was on him immediately, slashing downward with the fork again, then held up just as the tines pricked Long's skin.

'You'll talk quick and you'll talk straight,' Ben said softly, 'or this fork is going clean through your belly to your backbone.'

'All right,' Long howled. 'Just get the damn fork off of me.'

'I'll get it off when you talk,' Ben said, and pressed the fork a little harder against Long's belly.

'It happened a couple of weeks ago,' Long said, his wild eyes on Ben's face. 'Nosho showed up with his bunch at the post. They had 'bout twenty-five horses with 'em. Good animals, too. Probably stole 'em from some Mormon rancher in Utah. That pinto Nosho rides was in the bunch. He don't look like no race horse, so when Nosho offered to bet all of 'em against fifty guns, I took him up. I had a Ute kid riding my chestnut who's a purty good jockey, but the pinto ran off and left him.'

Ben stepped back, pulling the fork away from Long. He said, 'So you didn't pay off.'

'Hell no. Looked to me like my kid didn't try to make a race out of it. I fired the boy and told Nosho it wasn't a deal. They got mad and started for me, so I shot one of 'em. They pulled out then, but Nosho kept saying, "Me kill. Me kill." I figure Jack had given 'em orders not to

117

start nothing or they'd have beefed me then. Now that the shooting's started, they'll fix me good if they catch me.'

Ben jabbed the fork into the hay. 'You kill the brave you shot?'

'I dunno,' Long muttered. 'He was on his horse the last I seen of 'em.'

'You're a greedy fool,' Ben said angrily. 'You weren't satisfied with cheating 'em for the three years you've been on the river. You had to back out of a bet you'd lost and shoot one of 'em to boot.' He motioned toward the barn. 'Get out of my sight before I let 'em hang you.'

Long scrambled off the hay and grabbed up his rifle. He backed away, his gaze on Ben. 'You ain't turning me over to the Injuns?'

'It'd get us off the hook if we did, wouldn't it?' Ben shook his head. 'No, we won't turn you over to 'em.'

Long disappeared into the barn. Ben studied the brush along the river, unable to see anything except the cottonwoods and brush, but he was sure the Utes were there. Maybe not all of them. It seemed a good guess that Nosho had sent for reinforcements, but most of the band was probably hiding, watching and waiting for a chance to strike. Maybe at sundown when the light was too thin for accurate shooting, or tomorrow morning at dawn.

Ben stood motionless for a long time, thinking about this. When he measured the

118

worthless life of a man like Hank Long against the lives of the rest of the people who were here, he knew it would be a bad trade if it came to that. But could he bring himself to actually hand Long over to the Utes to be tortured to death?

No, he couldn't do it, he told himself, but he wasn't sure. The way it stood now, with Nosho having only eight or ten braves, Ben felt reasonably certain they could be beaten off; but suppose reinforcements came so there were forty or fifty in the band? He wasn't sure about it then. The more he thought about it, the less sure he was.

CHAPTER THIRTEEN

The afternoon was long and as nerve-wracking to Ben as the rasping sound of a file sharpening a saw. Up to the time the Utes had made their attack at Maudie's place, their threat had been little more than a menacing shadow. They had chased Justin Miles the day before, but they had not been seen again until this morning. Ben had hoped they had drifted away to look for easier scalps.

Now the threat was not the shadow but the substance. Ben knew the Indians were hiding in the willows. That they would attack sooner or later was a certainty, but he didn't know when or how or in what numbers. He wasn't even sure they would attack from the willows. It was possible they would slip around to the hill on the east and charge from the timber. He didn't really expect that, but rather than take any chances, he posted Bucky behind the house.

As he drifted back and forth between the house and the barn, he wondered how it was inside with the women. He wanted to see Cherry, but he didn't want to cross Maudie again. She was still in a temper, or had been at dinner time.

As soon as the men had finished eating Maudie had run all of them except Wheeler out of the house. She had refused to permit Long to come to the table to eat but had fixed a plate of food and poured a cup of coffee and told Bucky to take them to Long. It was just as well, Ben thought. The Utes knew Long was here, but they would probably shoot at him the instant he came into sight.

Wheeler stayed in the house after dinner to talk to Melissa. He was very thoughtful when he left. He started toward the river, then swung sharply toward the corral when Ben called to him. He grinned as he came up to Ben who was waiting beside his empty wagon.

'I know,' Wheeler said, his face red. 'They were just waiting for me. I'd have remembered what I was doing before I got there, but it might have been too late.'

'You don't have to see Indians like you did

120

this morning to know they're around,' Ben said. 'You can feel 'em, and you can smell 'em. Any Indian has got a lot of patience. He'll hunker down back of them willows and watch as long as he needs to. Maybe till Long shows himself and they get a chance to shoot him.'

Wheeler stood watching the willows and the occasional cottonwood that rose like a sprawling giant above the brush. 'I don't see a thing, Ben. I guess I don't feel and smell as well as you do.'

'Don't you get a hair-crawling feeling all over,' Ben said, 'just standing out here in the open and knowing they're hiding and watching you?'

'No, but it's not because I'm a brave man,' Wheeler said. 'I was scared this morning when I was in the potato patch and they were barreling down on us. I was so glad to get out of there I didn't care if Bucky ran the horses to death.' He shook his head again. 'But it's different here. You wouldn't want a prettier scene to look at than this. Or a more peaceful one.'

'That's what's wrong,' Ben said. 'It's too peaceful. Look real close. Nothing's moving. No birds flying. No rabbits scurrying around. It's a kind of deadly peacefulness that makes my skin crawl because I know they're watching me and could take a shot at me any time they want to.'

Wheeler cuffed back his black hat and

scratched his head thoughtfully. 'I'm ignorant, Ben. An ignorant man who doesn't know he's in danger isn't scared.'

'You know now that I've told you,' Ben said.

Wheeler pointed to his head. 'I know up here.' Then he tapped his chest. 'But not here. It's like talking about going to heaven or hell when you die. I can tell you about the danger of losing your soul and you can believe me, but it doesn't really change your life until you've had a saving experience.' He tapped his chest again. 'Then you feel it here and you know. You really know.'

Ben smiled. 'You are a preacher, Dave. You don't work like one and you don't act like one but once in a while you talk like one. That reminds me. Cherry and me want you to marry us. I don't know when but it'll be soon.'

'I'll be glad to,' Wheeler said. 'Marrying two people who are in love is one of the most satisfying things a preacher can do.' He paused, staring at the gold streaks made by the quaking aspens in the spruce on the ridge to the west. Finally he went on, 'I had completely forgotten about our danger when I left the house a few minutes ago. That was why I stupidly started walking without even thinking about where I was walking. Melissa had just told me about herself and Rick. She asked me for advice, but I didn't know what to say to her. I still don't.'

'I guess we've all got our problems,' Ben

said. 'Looks like my big one is gonna be Justin Miles when this is over with and Cherry and me are married.'

Wheeler nodded agreement. 'Justin Miles is a problem to all of us. You see, when Rick ran away with Melissa, he stole all his father's money. She says they can't go home because his father would put him in prison and her mother would kill her. She may be exaggerating it, but what she wanted advice about was Miles's farm. She thinks she and Rick ought to work for somebody this winter and save the money, but he wants to buy a place and Miles is trying to sell his to Rick, sight unseen.'

'The cheating old fraud,' Ben said. 'I don't suppose he told Bradley the Indians had burned his buildings.'

'No, I'm sure he didn't,' Wheeler said. 'About all the advice I could give her was to tell her to go back and face the music and return the stolen money, but she wouldn't listen. I don't know what else to say.'

'I know what I'll tell Justin,' Ben said angrily. 'I'll tell him I'm going to twist his thieving neck for him.'

'No, you'll just make things worse for Cherry and you,' Wheeler said. 'He told Rick he had to leave here as soon as the Indian scare was over because Cherry and you were getting married.'

'I supposed he was figuring on moving in

with us,' Ben said. 'The old goat's got more sense than I gave him credit for.'

'People don't always behave the way you think they will,' Wheeler said. 'I didn't know I had a murderous streak in me till I told Miles this morning I'd kill him if he brought that rope.'

'I figure you'd have done it, too,' Ben said. 'If you hadn't I would. It was the only way to handle the situation.' He started to turn away, then he said, 'We'll take the same guard duty we had last night except that I'll take Justin with me and let Bradley sleep. I trust him less all the time.'

'So do I after what Melissa said.' Wheeler yawned. 'If you don't need me, I'll crawl up on that haystack and think a while. I might even sleep some.'

'Go ahead,' Ben said. 'Just so I know where you are if we need you.'

'I'll be here,' Wheeler said. 'I sure don't intend to start walking again.'

When Ben moved around the house to ask Bucky if he had seen anything in the timber to the east, he found Justin Miles and Rick Bradley sitting on the wood pile talking. They stopped the instant they saw him and sat watching him.

He was strongly tempted to tell Miles what he thought of him, but he held his tongue. Wheeler was right. Anything Ben said would make things worse when he and Cherry were

124

married. He went on to where Bucky hunkered in the grass whittling on a chunk of aspen. The sight of Justin Miles and Bradley turned his temper sour.

'Anything doing?' Ben asked Bucky.

'Naw,' the boy answered. 'You've got a wrong hunch. They ain't on this side.'

'Maybe not,' Ben said irritably, 'only you're mighty damn smart when you can figure out what a bunch of Indians will do.'

Bucky's face turned red. 'I'm sorry, Ben. I ain't that smart.'

When Ben walked back, he saw that Miles and Bradley were still watching him closely, and again he was reminded of two school boys plotting to put something over on a teacher. He started toward them, feeling like knocking their heads together. When he reached them, he saw they were uneasy as if suspecting he intended to do some head knocking.

'Justin, you'll stand guard with me tonight,' Ben said. 'We'll take it from midnight till morning. Bradley, you can sleep till daylight. I don't trust you worth a damn at night.'

Miles started to argue, then closed his mouth without saying a word, but Bradley was insulted. He said, 'I could take guard duty alone and you know it, but it don't make no never mind to me whether you trust me or not. I don't trust you, neither. And another thing. I'm going to sleep in the house with my wife tonight so I can take care of her.'

'Try it,' Ben said. 'Maudie will tear you into little pieces if you do.'

He walked away, surprised to realize he felt sorry for both of them. In his way Justin Miles loved Cherry and would miss her. If there was a fight with the Utes, and Ben didn't doubt but what there would be, Miles would hold up his end.

Rick Bradley was something else. As far as Ben could see, there was nothing good in him. A boy who would rob his father and put Melissa through the torture he had on their way here was worthless in Ben's book. All of Bradley's tough talk did not change Ben's opinion. He was wind. Nothing more.

Ben put Miles and Bradley out of his mind because he had to make a decision about Hank Long. He had made it and yet he hadn't. When he let himself think how much he loved Cherry, he told himself he would not trade her life for a man as vicious as Hank Long.

Too, he thought of Bucky with his whole life before him; Wheeler, who could do so much for this valley if he stayed; Melissa, who would probably grow up into a fine woman; Maudie, who might have saved their lives if he had let her hang Long, did not deserve to die because he, Ben Holt, had kept her from committing murder. Even Bradley and Justin Miles were exemplary citizens compared to Hank Long.

Ben had never faced anything as complicated as this before in his life. He wasn't sure that giving Long up to the Utes would save them. He wasn't sure, either, that if the Utes made an attack, any of the whites would be killed, but the odds were that some of them would. When he came right down to the final decision, the thought of sending Long out to certain torture and death was so repugnant to him that he could not seriously consider it.

When Maudie called supper and Dave Wheeler slid off the haystack rubbing his eyes, Ben was no nearer to a decision than he had been when he had started to wrestle with the problem.

Long remained inside the barn and Miles stood guard while the rest ate supper. Melissa and Cherry were as pleasant and cheerful as ever, but Maudie was silent and tightlipped. She remained by the stove as the girls waited on the men.

When the meal was finished and the men rose, Maudie said, 'Mr Wheeler, I want to talk to you. Ben, you might as well hear it, too.'

Ben nodded. He said, 'Bradley, you stay with Bucky till you're relieved.'

Rick Bradley shrugged and followed Bucky outside, saying nothing about the order. Maudie stalked into the front room and waited until Ben and Wheeler sat down. Ben was uneasy because he knew he had humiliated Maudie. Normally she got over her 'mads' in a few minutes, but this time she was still hostile after more than half a day had passed.

Wheeler showed no uneasiness whatever. Ben, glancing at him, felt a great admiration for him. Maybe he'd had the wrong impression of preachers, but one thing was sure, Dave Wheeler did not fit the image Ben had of them.

'What is it, Mrs Kregg?' Wheeler asked.

She stood in the middle of the room, big arms folded over ponderous breasts. Sweat ran down her weather-beaten face, although Rick Bradley, the last to leave the house, had left the front door open and a cool wind was blowing into the room.

Maudie moistened her lips, then she burst out, 'You two think I'm just a big old cow wanting to fight all the time and trying to ... to run everything. You think that because I wanted to hang Hank Long I'm chuckful of meanness and hate and ... and everything.'

'Those are your thoughts, Mrs Kregg,' Wheeler said. 'Don't put your thoughts into my head and blame me for thinking them.'

She was shocked and surprised. She dropped into a chair and stared at Wheeler and then at Ben and finally brought her gaze back to Wheeler. She demanded, 'How did you know that?'

'I had a feeling,' he said. 'Mrs Kregg, you are a very impressive woman. You have an indomitable spirit. Beyond any doubt you are the most capable woman I ever met. You may deny this, but you have a great capacity for love. I've seen it in the way you feel about

128

Bucky and I saw it again in the way you took care of Melissa. It is too bad that you let hate possess you the way it did this morning. You see, love unites you with God, but hate drives you away from Him.'

She blinked as she considered what he'd said, then she demanded, 'You thought a lot of Nathan Meeker, didn't you?'

'Yes, I did,' Wheeler said sadly. 'He was in many ways a saintly man. I find myself close to tears whenever I think about what must have happened to him.'

'Well then,' she said, 'don't you hate the Indians?'

'No,' Wheeler said. 'I can't afford to. I know what hate does to people and what it will do to me. There are many sins that man can be guilty of, but the worst is to let yourself be separated from God.'

She thought about that, then slowly turned her head to look at Ben. 'Them devils are after Long mostly, ain't they?'

'That's the way I've got it sized up,' he said.

'It'd save our hides if you gave him up, wouldn't it?'

'I think so,' Ben answered. 'I don't know for sure, Maudie. I've been trying all afternoon to figure it out. Right now there ain't enough of 'em out yonder to wipe us out, but suppose a big bunch rides in tonight? We'd be in for it then.' He glanced at Wheeler, then at Maudie. 'Would you give him up to save our hides?'

'No, I reckon not.' She rose and turned toward the kitchen. 'Send Long in and I'll give him his supper. Justin, too.'

When Ben and Wheeler were outside, the preacher said, 'She had to talk it out. She didn't want us to think she was wicked or something, so she was ready to defend herself.'

'She was on the prod there at first,' Ben said, 'but you pulled her teeth real good. Stay here and tell Justin to go in and eat. I'll get Long.'

The light was too thin for the Indians watching from the river to recognize Long as he moved from the barn to the house, but if he was grateful for being permitted to go into the house for his supper he did not show it. Ben guessed he was afraid to face Maudie, and told himself Long had a right to be.

When Ben returned to where Wheeler waited in front of the house, he said, 'This is a life and death proposition, Dave. Maudie knows it, though I don't suppose anybody else but Long has figured it out. You're a smart man, so I'll let...'

'Wait a minute,' Wheeler interrupted. 'I don't pretend to be a smart man. I haven't figured out yet just what I should say to Melissa.'

'Let's see what you say to me,' Ben said. 'If Long wasn't here, I think the Utes would drift on looking for easier sport somewhere else, but they never forgive a man who's done what he did to 'em. He backed out on a bet and shot one

130

of them. Maybe killed him. Long claims he ain't sure. None of the Utes like Justin, but they won't risk their lives to get him, and they've got nothing against the rest of us. You heard what Maudie said. What do you say?'

'It didn't rain,' Wheeler said, 'so it looks to me like it wouldn't be hard to burn the house. The barn, too. Once we were in the open, they'd get all of us, wouldn't they?'

'We'd have a hell of a time defending ourselves,' Ben admitted.

'I don't want to die and I know you don't,' Wheeler said. 'I can't even let myself think of the Indians making the women prisoners, but we'd never be proud of ourselves if we gave Long up. I don't think we can do it.'

'I keep telling myself the same,' Ben said, 'then I get a picture in my mind of Cherry. I can see them raping her and Melissa, and killing both girls later by torturing them to death. I tell you, Dave, Hank Long's miserable, stinking life just ain't worth it.'

Wheeler hadn't been listening. He was staring into the near darkness toward the river, his hand dropping onto Ben's arm. He squeezed it, saying in a low tone, 'Ben, something's moving out there.'

Ben whirled. He saw them, too, half a dozen vague shapes worming their way across the grass toward the corral. He knew then, in that heart-stopping moment, that the question

131

about handing Long over to the Indians was no longer a question.

CHAPTER FOURTEEN

Ben had that one short moment when he couldn't breathe. He felt a knife-like stab of pain shoot deep down into his belly. The Utes were finally making their try for the horses. For Long, too, probably thinking he was still in the barn.

There might be more of them, working their way across the grass from some other direction. If they were, they would be hidden from him by the barn and haystacks. One thing was sure. The closer they got to the barn and corral before they were discovered, the better their chance of success.

Then the moment of paralysis passed. He brought the Winchester to his shoulder and fired, and as he squeezed the trigger, he remembered that Bucky was alone at the barn except for Rick Bradley who was worse than nothing.

'Indians,' Ben yelled, and raced across the yard. He thought he had hit the closest Ute. The brave yelled and jumped to his feet and whirled and ran. Ben couldn't see exactly what was happening, the light being thin and running as hard as he was, but he had the feeling that the Indians who had been out there

132

on their bellies in the grass had started back toward the river.

It wasn't really an attack at all, he thought. They had hoped to get close before they were discovered, and now that they had been seen, they were getting out.

An instant later he realized he was dead wrong. He heard Bucky yell and heard him shoot. A split second later two Utes appeared out of the dusk and lunged toward the corral gate. Ben fired at the first one and saw him go down. Another Indian was inside the corral chasing the horses around the inclosure, yelling at them and apparently expecting the Utes on the other side of the gate to open it.

The second Indian, who was just behind the one Ben had shot, rushed at him. He caught a glimpse of a steel blade in the brave's hand and instinctively wheeled aside. The knife flashed by, slashing the sleeve of his left arm and opening a shallow wound. He had no time to shoot, so he brought the barrel of the rifle down in a numbing blow that caught the Indian on the neck and spilled him forward flat on his face.

Ben didn't wait to see whether he had killed the two braves or not. Bucky was struggling with a third one by the corner of the barn. He heard Wheeler firing from in front of the house, then the boom of Maudie's Sharps, but the shooting seemed far away and of no importance. Even as he plunged toward

133

Bucky, he had the terrifying feeling he was too late.

Luckily the warrior Bucky was fighting was a small one. He might even have been a boy Bucky's age. He was trying to stab Bucky with a knife, but Bucky had a grip on his wrist and the Indian couldn't twist free.

They were straining and grunting and kicking up a cloud of dust when Ben reached them. He couldn't risk shooting, as close as they were, so again he used his rifle barrel as a club, bringing it down in a short, chopping blow on the Ute's head. Ben stumbled back as the Indian who was inside the corral yelled something. The brave who had been fighting Bucky turned and ran. Ben fired at him, but apparently missed. At least the Indian was out of the fight, for he kept running until he disappeared in the thinning light.

It was over that quickly. Ben wheeled back toward the corral gate. The two Indians he had put down were gone. The horses inside the corral were still milling around, but not as hard as they had been, so the warrior who had been chasing them must have left.

Ben turned to Bucky who had backed up to the wall of the barn and leaned against it, panting hard. 'You all right?' Ben asked.

'I guess so,' Bucky said, 'except for being scared. He almost got me.'

Maudie let go with the Sharps again. Then Wheeler appeared beside Ben, asking, 'Either one of you hurt?'

'I got a scratch on my arm,' Ben said.

Long and Justin Miles were firing from the front of the house. Ben, looking toward the river, couldn't see any of the Indians. He yelled, 'They're gone.' He turned to Wheeler. 'You think you hit any of 'em?'

'I doubt it,' Wheeler said. 'It's too dark to get a bead on them. They were pretty smart, too, zig-zagging back and forth.'

Maudie and Cherry ran toward the barn, Long and Miles following. Suddenly Ben thought of Rick Bradley. He asked Bucky, 'Did any of 'em get into the barn?'

'No,' he said. 'I was right by the door when I first seen all three of 'em. I took a shot, but I must have missed. The one who tackled me was in the lead. The other two went for the corral gate.'

Maudie lumbered up, blowing hard. She managed to ask between puffs, 'You hurt, Bucky?'

'Naw, I'm all right,' the boy answered.

Cherry and the two men were there then. Ben caught Cherry by an arm. 'We're all fine,' he said. 'You get back to the house, all of you.' He pulled Cherry close to him, saying in a low tone, 'Where's Melissa?'

'She was in the bedroom when the shooting started,' Cherry said.

'Keep her in the house,' Ben said, and gave Cherry a push. 'Go on back, all of you. Finish your supper, Hank. You, too, Justin.'

Cherry obeyed, but Long and Miles stood there not knowing what was in Ben's mind. Maudie looked Bucky over, then turned to Ben. 'Bucky says you got a cut. Come inside and we'll look at it.'

'I'll be there in a minute,' Ben said. 'Damn it, will you do what I tell you?'

Long and Miles returned to the house, but Maudie stood her ground, demanding, 'What's the matter with you, Ben? You got some of 'em penned up in the barn that you want to handle personally?'

'Yeah, ten of 'em,' Ben snapped, then he had his temper under control and said, 'I can't figure out what's happened to Bradley. Anyhow, I don't want Melissa coming out here till we know, so I thought it'd be better if you were all back in the house and could tell her it was over and nobody was hurt.'

'You must have some notion of what happened to him,' Maudie said stubbornly.

'We're going to look for him,' Ben said in exasperation. 'Maudie, will you please get the hell out of here?'

She grunted something and finally turned and walked back to the house. When she was gone, Wheeler said, 'You think he's inside?'

'We'll see,' Ben said. 'You stay here, Bucky. I don't think they'll be back, but we can't take any chances.'

Ben and Wheeler went into the barn, Ben

pulling the door shut. He struck a match and lighted a lantern that he took down from a peg near the door. He called, 'Bradley.'

No answer. Both men stood motionless for a moment, then Ben heard what sounded like someone crying. He nodded at Wheeler and they walked along the runway to the back stall. There they found him, lying face down in the litter, his shoulders shaking in a violent paroxysm of sobbing.

Wheeler knelt beside Bradley. He asked, 'What's the matter, Rick?'

Bradley pretended he didn't hear. He didn't look up or seem to be aware of their presence. Wheeler put a hand on his shoulder. 'Rick, this is Dave Wheeler. What's the matter?'

He shook off Wheeler's hand. 'Lemme alone,' he muttered. 'I ain't going out there. You can't make me.'

'He's yellow,' Ben said. 'Clean yellow right down to his heels. Grab that shoulder, Dave. Let's get him to his feet.'

They hauled him upright and shoved him back against the wall of the stall. He had rolled around in the horse manure and had soiled himself. Now he propped himself upright, his head lolling back and forth, his chin against his chest.

Ben looked at him, thinking how Bucky had fought like a man, Bucky who was four or five years younger than Rick Bradley and much smaller. A crazy rage took hold of Ben and he

137

drew a hand back to slap Bradley across the face, but Wheeler caught his arm.

'No, Ben,' Wheeler said. 'You go tell Melissa he's all right. I'll stay and talk with him.'

Slobber ran down Bradley's chin. He muttered, 'I wanta see Melissa.'

'No,' Wheeler said. 'You're not fit to see her.'

Without a word Ben walked out of the barn. If he had stayed, he would have lost control of his temper. Bucky asked, 'He's in there, ain't he?'

'Yeah, he's there,' Ben said. 'Well son, you are a hell of a good man. I'm proud of you. So is Maudie.'

Bucky sucked in a long breath. 'I dunno 'bout that, Ben. I've been scared ever since Carl Niven brought the word.'

'Funny thing,' Ben said. 'Being scared makes you fight like the devil, and it turns Rick Bradley into a rabbit. Stay here. I'll send Long and Justin out as soon as they finish eating.'

Ben went across the yard to the house, wondering what he would tell Melissa. How could Rick Bradley face her or any of them after this? Maybe he could cover up with more big talk and Melissa might believe him, but no one else would.

The instant he stepped through the front door Melissa ran to him and gripped his arms. 'Where's Rick? Is he all right?' Then she saw the dried blood on Ben's left arm and she cried,

138

'Rick's hurt and you won't tell me. I'm going to him.'

'No, you're staying in the house,' Ben said. 'He's not hurt. I give you my word.' She shrank away from him, her eyes wide and staring, and he repeated slowly, 'Rick is all right.'

'Then why won't you let me see him?' Melissa wailed. 'Ever since we got here, you or Mrs Kregg or somebody has kept us apart. A wife belongs with her husband.'

'Not when there's a war to be fought,' Ben said, 'and that's what we've got. A war! A woman's job is to take care of things in the house and see that the men are fed. You've got to leave the fighting to the men.'

She turned away and dabbed at her eyes, then she whirled to face him. 'All right, I'll do my share of the work inside and Rick will do the fighting. He said all the time that if he had a gun, he'd run the Indians back onto the reservation. You did give him a gun, didn't you?'

Ben hesitated, knowing he could not tell her the truth. Sooner or later she would have to hear it, but a lie would do for the moment. Maybe later Maudie or Cherry could tell her.

'Yes, we gave him a gun,' Ben said.

Maudie was standing a few feet behind Melissa. Now she stepped forward and put an arm around the girl. She said, 'You've had a hard day and it'll be a long time before you'll get your strength back. You'd better come to bed.'

The girl went with Maudie into the bedroom. She kept looking back at Ben as if expecting him to tell her something else, but he said nothing until Maudie closed the door. Then he jerked his head at Hank Long and Justin Miles who had come into the room from the kitchen.

'I've got Bucky watching out by the barn,' Ben said, 'but you two better go help him. I'll be out as soon as Cherry fixes my arm.'

The men obeyed, both plainly curious about Rick Bradley, but neither asked about him. Cherry took Ben's hand and led him into the kitchen. She had him sit down, brought a pan of hot water from the stove, rags, and a bottle of whisky and set them on the table. She washed the wound, poured whisky over it, then bandaged it.

Cherry sat down beside him. She said, 'Melissa is just a child, Ben. She got so tired on the trip and was so hungry she's sick. What's going to happen to her?'

'I don't know what's going to happen to either one of them,' Ben said. He told her how he and Wheeler had found Bradley, then asked, 'What will Melissa do when she finds out? She can't go on believing in him and making excuses for him, can she?'

'I don't know that, either,' Cherry said. 'Maudie has talked about taking Melissa in, but she wouldn't have Rick around the place

140

and I don't suppose Melissa will leave him.'

They sat motionless for a time, thinking about Melissa and Rick, then Ben said, 'Your pa has been trying to sell his place to Bradley.'

Cherry shook her head in disgust. 'I'm not surprised. Well, in the morning I'll tell Melissa it wasn't worth what Pa's asking when the buildings were there.' She hesitated, studying Ben's face, then she asked, 'What were the Indians trying to do? And is this likely to be the end of it?'

'They were purty tricky,' he said. 'Tricky enough to fool me. There were six of 'em in front, but looks to me like they was just decoys. I suppose they expected us to chase 'em. Anyhow, they had four more sneaking in from another direction. I didn't see 'em come in, so I don't know where they came from, but they were the ones who were supposed to get the horses. Long, too, maybe. I couldn't tell about that.'

He wiped a hand across his face and shook his head. His arm hurt, he was dead tired, and he was sleepy. 'I don't know if that's the end of it or not, but it won't be if they get reinforcements.' He rose. 'Honey, I'm going to get some sleep.'

He kissed her, then he said, 'I spoke to Dave Wheeler about marrying us. I didn't tell him when. I just said soon.'

She nodded and smiled. 'I want it to be soon, Ben. Real soon.'

When he left the house, the thought came to him that the siege might last for days. He wondered how long he could stand it, with Dave Wheeler the only man he could really depend on.

CHAPTER FIFTEEN

Ben and Justin Miles relieved Wheeler and Bucky at midnight. Miles was cranky and tired and sleepy, but he moved across the yard to the house without arguing, his rifle in his right hand.

'Anything happen?' Ben asked Wheeler.

'No,' the preacher said. Bucky went into the barn, but Wheeler stood there scratching his chin. Finally he said,

'Ben, I know I'm boogery. After what happened this evening, it seemed to me that every shadow was a Ute waiting to knife me. I heard all kinds of things in the darkness, so it's hard to know what was real and what was imagination.'

Ben could not make out the man's expression in the darkness, but he sensed that something was bothering him. He prodded, 'What's eating on you, Dave? It's more'n imagination, ain't it?'

'I think so,' Wheeler answered. 'It happened about an hour ago. I was over yonder by the

142

haystack when I thought I heard someone run past the corral. I was too startled to do anything for a moment, then I thought it couldn't be an Indian. I told myself I wouldn't have heard anything if it had been.'

'Bucky didn't hear it?'

'No, but that doesn't prove anything,' Wheeler answered. 'I asked him right away, but he'd been circling the house and was behind it.'

'Well, it wasn't me or Justin,' Ben said thoughtfully. 'Bradley wouldn't be out there, and Long sure ain't gonna take no chances with the Indians wanting him like they do.'

Wheeler sucked in a long breath. 'Just my nerves, I guess. Seems like each hour gets a little tougher. I didn't expect anything easy when I left home, but I didn't look for anything like this, either. Poor Nathan! I wish we knew for sure what happened to him and the rest of the white people at the agency.'

'We know,' Ben said.

'I guess so,' Wheeler said. 'It's just that I have to keep hoping they're alive.'

He disappeared into the barn. Ben walked around the corral and threaded his way through the haystacks, knowing exactly what Wheeler had meant when he'd said it seemed that every shadow was a Ute waiting for him.

Every half hour or so Ben checked on Miles and found him awake and moving and frankly admitting he was frightened. He seemed to find

143

some satisfaction in Ben's remark that only a fool would not be scared with a situation like this. Too, he found assurance in Ben's certainty that the Utes would not make a move before dawn.

'I'll get Bradley and Long out here by that time,' Ben told him. 'There's about an hour when it begins to get light that's the most likely time for them to try again.'

They wore out the long hours, moving and then stopping to listen and moving again. The more Ben thought about the Bradleys and Long, the more he resented their presence. He owed nothing to any of them, they ate up his food and their horses ate his hay and none of the three was of any real help.

Long did have a rifle and was a good shot. On the other hand, it was his presence that created a pressing danger for all of them. Any way that Ben looked at it, the rest would be better off without them.

How much is a man his brother's keeper? Ben thought about it as the slow minutes dragged by. He would agree that in principle he was his brother's keeper and Dave Wheeler would have said that was right, but Ben did not agree that he was obliged to look out for two children like Rick and Melissa Bradley who never should have left home in the first place, or a rascal like Hank Long who was a disgrace to the white race.

The hard fact remained that they were here.

He wouldn't like it, but he knew he would continue to feed the Bradleys and use some of his valuable hay that might leave him short next spring. Liking it or not, he still could not bring himself to actually turn Long over to the Utes even if he were certain it would save the rest of them.

Presently the first dawn light began working into the sky above the mountains to the east. In a way he was relieved. They had made it through the second night. On the other hand, he had reason to be more apprehensive than ever. The next hour was crucial. If the Utes made an attack today, it would probably come within this hour.

Ben circled the haystacks and turned toward the barn. His natural optimism asserted itself. They had beaten off one attack with his shallow arm wound the only casualty. The chances were good that if they lived through today and tonight, they would be all right. The relief party from Fort Steele should arrive on the Yampa by Friday, or Saturday at the latest.

As soon as the relief column crossed the river, the raiding bands of Utes like Nosho's would drift back onto the reservation. Probably all of them would withdraw from Milk Creek. Whether they had wiped out what was left of Thornburgh's command or not, Ben was sure they would not stand and fight a bigger relief party.

Ben grinned in self-derision as he opened the

barn door, knowing that he might well be fooling himself with this optimistic thinking. The relief party could be many days reaching the Yampa. The group that had sought refuge here on his ranch could not survive that long. The food would be used up. The hay would be gone. Maudie would decide to take Bucky and go home. Rick Bradley would do something completely wild and irresponsible.

The truth was that anything could happen. They had one day, maybe two. That was all. Then the tension that gripped them would tear them apart like a giant fly wheel that kept increasing its speed as it turned until it disintegrated.

He shook Long awake and told him to take his rifle and go outside, then went on to the last stall where he expected to find Rick Bradley. The boy wasn't there. He wasn't anywhere in the barn.

Ben stepped outside and shut the door. He asked Long who was standing close to the wall, 'When did Bradley leave?'

'I didn't know he had,' Long answered, 'but I sure wasn't paying no attention to him. I was sleeping.'

Ben walked slowly to the house. The light deepened as the stars died, the sky gradually changing from night black to day blue. There would probably be no rain today, Ben thought, and found himself shivering. The breeze, chilled by its passage across the peaks, held a

146

sharp bite. The first killing frost of fall was not far away.

Ben's mind did not linger on the weather for more than a moment. He was concerned about Rick Bradley, but he could make no sense of the boy's disappearance. Ben could not believe that young Bradley had left the safety of the barn of his own accord. Still, that had to be what had happened for no one had forced him to leave. But where had he gone?

He might have slipped into the house. Maybe he'd sat down in the kitchen and fallen asleep. It was a crazy notion, but Ben had to make sure. He strode around the house and through the back door. Even in the thin dawn light Ben saw that the room was empty.

Unless Bradley had been driven out of his mind by the frenzy of fear he had experienced during the raid, Ben told himself that it was unreasonable to think he would have left the barn. No, it was more than unreasonable; it was unthinkable. It was ridiculous the way his thoughts returned to this conclusion. He was tempted to return to the barn and look again for Bradley, but there was no sense in that. He had made sure Rick Bradley was not in the barn.

Suddenly Ben remembered how furious Bradley was because he had not been allowed to sleep with Melissa. It was incredible that he would get into bed with his wife, knowing that Cherry was in the same bed, but Rick Bradley

147

was an incredible person. It occurred to Ben that he kept thinking in terms of words like incredible, unreasonable, and unthinkable. Well, they applied to the situation, he told himself, and to Bradley, too.

As Ben stepped into the front room he remembered Dave Wheeler saying that Melissa was a balance wheel for her husband. He remembered, too, how incoherent Bradley had been last night. In his confused state, he might have thought of nothing except the uncontrollable desire to be comforted by Melissa.

Maudie sat upright in bed, her massive jaw jutting out belligerently. 'Now what the hell are you doing here this time of night? Ain't a woman got the right...'

'Oh, shut up,' Ben said wearily. 'I'm here because there's something I want you to do. Go into the bedroom and see if Bradley's in there. I can't find him.'

Outraged, Maudie snapped, 'I ain't getting up and parading around in front of you in my nightgown. Besides, I can tell you he ain't there. Cherry would scratch his eyes out if he tried it.'

'She sure would if she was awake,' Ben said, 'but she's so worn out she might sleep through anything. Now go see if he's there.'

She sat up on the edge of the bed and glared at Ben. 'I don't see why you want to look for him if he's gone. I say good riddance to bad

148

rubbish.'

'We've got to explain it to Melissa if he's gone,' Ben said. 'Besides, it don't make any sense. He knew he was safe inside the barn unless we got wiped out or it was burned, so I just don't savvy him walking out where an Indian might be waiting to knife him.'

Maudie, fully awake now, grunted something to indicate she saw the point. She got up and padded across the room to the bedroom door; she opened it a crack, looked in, and eased the door shut.

She came back to where Ben was standing in the middle of the room. 'He ain't there. I knowed he wouldn't be, but by glory, this is funny.' She paused, then she said, 'Ben, my husband used to tell me about prospectors who got lost in the mountains. If they was greenhorns, they'd get panicky. They'd lose their heads and start to run in any direction and they'd go plumb loony. He said sometimes they'd have to throw their hats into the creek to tell which way it was running.'

Ben nodded thoughtfully. 'You're trying to tell me he was so scared he was crazy and just wandered off?'

'That's it,' Maudie said. 'The first time I seen that boy I knowed there wasn't a solid bone in his body. Just hot air. That's all he is. Melissa had a bad home, but she didn't do nothing to help herself when she married him.'

'Get dressed,' Ben said. 'I'm not gonna chase

149

through the quakies looking for him, but I ain't real satisfied, neither.'

He went out through the front door, calling, 'Justin.'

Miles appeared from the side of the house, asking, 'Anything wrong?'

'Yeah, something's wrong,' Ben said. 'Rick Bradley's gone. You done a lot of talking to him yesterday. I've got a hunch you know more about him than anybody here.'

'Now you just hold your hosses,' Miles said hotly. 'If he walked out, I didn't have nothing to do with it and I dunno where he went or why. All I know is he ain't dry behind the ears, which same you know as well as I do.'

'What were you two talking about so much yesterday?' Ben demanded.

Miles shifted the rifle from one hand to the other. He cleared his throat, staring at Ben's face in the dim light as if trying to decide whether he was going to be scolded. Finally he said, 'Rick wanted to buy a place here in the valley, and I knowed I had to get out, you and Cherry getting married and not wanting me underfoot. Not that I blame you, you understand. No young couple likes to have a father-in-law around all the time. Well, I offered to sell him my place for five hundred dollars and you know that's dirt cheap.'

'You tell him the Indians burned your buildings?'

'No.' Miles shifted his weight and dug a boot

150

toe into the dirt. 'Fact is, I dunno they did.'

'Maybe he sneaked out to see for himself.'

'Are you loco?' Miles demanded. 'He was so scared of an Indian fight he wouldn't have left the barn if it was burning down around him.'

Ben wheeled and strode toward the barn. Miles was right. Bradley wouldn't have left the safety of the barn under any circumstances. Still, the fact was he had. Ben woke Wheeler. When they were outside, the preacher rubbing his eyes and trying to wake up, Ben told him about Bradley's absence.

Wheeler walked to the horse trough and sloshed water over his face. He turned back to Ben. 'I'm sorry. I feel like I'd been drugged and hit on the head or something.' He scrubbed his face with both hands and walked back and forth for a moment, then he turned to look at Ben.

'It must have been Rick I heard last night,' Wheeler said finally. 'I didn't think of it at the time or even when I told you about it, but there is something I should have told you. When I was talking to him after you left, he kept saying he was going to run away. He said he didn't come here for the Indians to torture him. Well, he was more or less incoherent and most of what he said didn't make any sense, so I didn't give it much serious thought. Now I know I should have because that's certainly what he's done.'

'He must have been completely crazy,' Ben

151

said. 'I've known fear to do that to people.'

Wheeler nodded. 'To weak people, and Rick was about the weakest person I ever ran into. Now even if the Utes don't get him, he'll kill himself trying to get away.'

'That's just about what he'll...' Ben began.

'Ben,' Miles shouted, running toward him. 'It ain't very light yet, but take a look out yonder. Is that Bradley?'

Ben and Wheeler turned. The sun was not up yet, and a faint mist was blowing toward them from the river, but there was enough light to make out something lying in the grass about halfway between the ford and the house. At first Ben thought it was a pile of rags, but he knew at once it wasn't. It was Rick Bradley's body.

'I'm going out there and bring him in,' Wheeler said.

'No.' Ben grabbed his arm. 'Don't be a fool.'

'He might be alive,' Wheeler said. 'If he is, perhaps we can do something for him. Even if he's not, we can't leave him out there. Melissa will see him. She'll probably run to him and get killed. This is the time to bring him in before it gets full daylight.'

Wheeler tried to jerk free, but Ben refused to release his grip. The thought raced through his mind that he was not his brother's keeper, that Rick Bradley was dead and it didn't make any difference where the corpse was. Wheeler pawed at him angrily and said to let go, but Ben held on. If anyone had a chance to bring the body in Ben knew he was the man, and that, he guessed, made him his brother's keeper.

'I'll do it,' Ben said.

'No, no,' Wheeler shouted. 'We can't afford to lose you. My loss wouldn't be important either way.'

Ben knew there was no use to argue with a man as stubborn as David Wheeler once he had made up his mind. The preacher was right about one thing. This was the time to bring the body in, with the light still thin and the mist rising from the river.

Wheeler turned, apparently thinking Ben had agreed to let him go, but as he swung around Ben hit him, a sledging upper-cut that caught him on the point of the chin and knocked him down as effectively as if Ben had hit him with a club. He lay motionless, out cold.

'Keep him here, Justin,' Ben said, and started across the grass toward the river.

Ben had not taken ten strides until half a dozen rifles opened up from the willows along the river, powder flame making red, jagged streaks in the early morning light, the crashing sound of the shots rolling out across the valley.

'Come back, you fool,' Miles yelled. 'He ain't worth it even if he's alive.'

Ben stopped and threw his rifle down. He had forgotten it was still in his right hand. He watched the puffs of smoke that hung motionless in the still air, then drifted away. The slugs had dug into the ground ahead of him, giving him the distinct feeling that the shots had been meant for warnings. He didn't remember Nosho, but he had fed a number of Utes in the two years he had been here and very likely some of them were in Nosho's party.

Ben raised his hands to show he had dropped his Winchester. He yelled, 'Nosho, I'm not trying to fight you. I'm going to bring the white man's body in so we can bury it.'

He waited for fifteen or twenty seconds. The Utes didn't say anything. Nothing stirred in the brush. He walked slowly forward, his eyes on the body. He felt his heart hammering so violently he thought it would jump out of his chest. Every step he took might be his last. He had faced death many times, but never in a situation in which it seemed as certain as this.

Now that he had started, more or less on impulse, he could not turn back. Whatever happened, the Utes must never get the impression he was afraid, so he kept walking, slowly and deliberately, until he reached the body.

The sight was almost too much for him. Bradley's clothes had been torn and ripped, his body horribly mutilated, and as Ben stooped and picked him up, he thought that this was probably what had happened to Nathan Meeker and the rest of the whites who were at the agency.

154

Ben turned and started back, the slashed, bloody body in his arms. He forced himself to keep the same deliberate pace, knowing that a show of haste would be taken for fear and would break the spell. Once that spell had been broken, he would probably get a dozen rifle bullets in his back.

Wheeler, Miles, and Long were standing by the barn wall. Wheeler had recovered Ben's rifle. He held it in his left hand, his right massaging his jaw where Ben had hit him. Maudie crossed the yard and stood motionless beside the three men. They watched him in silence, all of them showing the concern and tension that gripped them except Hank Long who seemed indifferent.

For Ben the distance between where he had picked up the body and the corral was not measured by feet; it stretched into miles. The few minutes that it took him to cover the distance were hours. Then he was there; he laid the body down and wiped sweat from his face, realizing he was shaking as if he had a chill.

'You are a fool, Ben Holt,' Maudie said hotly. 'A blithering idiot. You need someone to run herd on you.'

After that no one said anything for a time. They stared in horror until Wheeler went into the barn and brought out a blanket with which he covered the body. Ben knew that dried blood smeared the front of his shirt, but right now a question was prodding him that was going to have to be answered.

'Who's going to tell Melissa?' Ben asked.

No one answered.

CHAPTER SIXTEEN

Cherry was sleepily aware that Maudie had opened the door and had glanced into the bedroom. She turned over, the rumble of talk coming to her from the front room. At first the words were not clear, and she was dropping off again when Ben's voice stirred her consciousness: 'I'm not gonna chase through the quakies looking for him, but I ain't real satisfied, neither.' He stomped out of the house and she heard him shout, 'Justin.'

Alarmed, she sat up and put her feet on the floor. She dressed quickly so she wouldn't wake Melissa, and for a moment stood looking at the girl. The room was warm, and Melissa had thrown back the quilt. She lay on her side in a little ball, her back to Cherry, her knees under her chin. In the thin dawn light, her blond hair seemed only a shade darker than the pillow.

Funny how people's relationship changed in a crisis, Cherry thought. In the few hours Melissa had been in this house, she had worked herself into the hearts of everyone. The people who knew her, even Ben and Bucky who didn't

156

know her very well, felt a great sympathy for her. Only Rick took her for granted and seemed to think her sole duty was to look after him.

Rick needed looking after, Cherry guessed. As she put her hair up, she thought that Melissa needed looking after, too, but Rick never thought of doing anything for her, not even such a simple thing as pleasing her by giving her a compliment.

Cherry decided that Rick Bradley was the most worthless human being she had ever seen in her life. She had thought that about her father, but at least he was not a coward and he was capable when he wanted to be. Rick, as far as she could see, was a coward, a braggart, and inept at everything. But what would Melissa do without him?

She gave her hair a final pat and slipped out of the bedroom. Maudie, who was dressed, stood in the front door. Cherry crossed to her, asking, 'What's wrong?'

'Everything's wrong,' Maudie whispered. 'If I had that damned worthless Rick in my hands, I'd shake him till his teeth rattled. Ben's gonna get himself killed because of that fool kid.'

'Ben?' Cherry pushed past Maudie to stand in front of the house. 'Where is he?'

She saw him then, a vague shape walking slowly toward the river. The next moment the morning exploded into violence, the jagged tongues of gunflame darting into the misty air from the brush along the river. She heard her father yell for Ben to come back; she saw Ben drop his rifle. He raised his hands, he shouted something at the Indians, and then went on.

They would kill him, she thought. An anguished cry broke out of her. She darted forward, expecting the Ute rifles to crash into the silence. Maudie, as big and ungainly as she was, moved faster and caught her by the arm and held her.

'Take it easy, honey,' Maudie said. 'You can't do no good out there. You'd just make it worse for Ben.'

Cherry turned and buried her face against Maudie's bosom. 'They'll kill Ben,' she whispered. 'Don't you see? They'll kill him.'

Maudie didn't say anything. She held Cherry and let her cry. Presently she said, 'I reckon they're gonna let Ben bring him in.'

Cherry whirled away from Maudie. She stood frozen as she watched Ben walk toward the corral, Rick's long body dangling from his arms. He moved slowly, so slowly that Cherry asked, 'Why doesn't he hurry?'

'He'd like to,' Maudie said. 'You can bet he'd like to, but he dasn't.'

Cherry stood in front of the house, her body rigid, her fists clenched so hard that the nails bit into her palms, the pressure against her chest making it hard to breathe. She saw Maudie cross the yard and join the men at the barn; she watched Ben until he reached the barn and laid

Rick's body on the ground. Even then she found it hard to breathe. She had never expected Ben to live this long.

Suddenly she could not stand it any longer. She ran to Ben, calling his name. He held out his arms and she fell into them, sobbing. When she could speak, she said, 'I was so sure they'd kill you.'

He laughed. 'You know, honey, I thought the same thing.'

She drew back, tears marring her vision as she looked at him. She blinked and squeezed her eyes shut, then opened them. She said, 'Ben, you're the bravest man I ever saw.'

For a crazy moment she thought he was going to cry, but he didn't. He said, 'No, I guess not.'

Maudie cleared her throat. 'I ain't one to lie to nobody, and I figger Rick getting himself killed is a good thing. He wasn't no good to himself or Melissa or us, but Ben's question has got to be answered. Who is going to tell Melissa?'

There was silence for a long moment, then Cherry said, 'How did it happen? What was Rick doing out there?'

'Nobody knows,' Wheeler answered, 'but he told me last night he was going to run away. He said he didn't come here for the Indians to torture him. I heard something when I was standing guard. It must have been him, slipping out of the barn.'

'But why?' Cherry asked. 'He wasn't running away. He went right toward them.'

'We'll never know,' Ben said, 'but it's a good guess that he was so panicky he didn't know what he was doing. All he could think of was getting away. He must have got turned around and thought he was going the other way.'

'We can't tell Melissa that,' Wheeler said. 'She knows some of his weaknesses, of course, but she was always overlooking them. I think she'll be happier if she never knows what a complete coward he was.' The preacher paused, looking at Maudie and then Cherry, and finally adding, 'I'll tell her if you think I'm the one to do it, but I honestly think it would be better if one of you women spoke to her first. Later on I believe I can be of some help.'

Bucky came out of the barn, his wide eyes fixed on the blanket-covered body. Ben said, 'Fetch me that canvas in the back stall, Bucky.' When the boy disappeared into the barn, Ben said, 'We'd best start digging a grave, but I don't think we'd better take time to build a coffin. We'll just roll him up in the canvas. Maybe the Utes won't do nothing after the way they let me come in with the body, but we'd still better keep our eyes open.'

'Sure we had,' Maudie said. 'The sooner we get the burying done, the better.'

Cherry forced herself to throw the blanket back and look at the body as Bucky handed the canvas to Ben. She turned away, thinking, *Ben could have been lying out there in the grass beside Rick.*

She began to tremble. She shut her eyes tightly, but she could not close out the mental image of Ben lying on the ground, blood soaking his shirt, his lips parted, the dried brown mask covering much of his face.

With her eyes still shut, she said, 'I'll tell Melissa. I guess I can do it better than anyone else because I know how she'll feel. There was a little while when that was the way I felt.'

Ben slipped an arm around her waist and hugged her. He said softly, 'I'm all right, honey.'

'I know, but Rick isn't.' Cherry moistened her lips, then she said slowly, 'It's like Maudie says. Melissa is better off without Rick, but I can't tell her that. Maybe she never will understand about him.'

'No, I don't think she will,' Wheeler said. 'She felt responsible for him and she'll blame herself because he's dead.'

Cherry started toward the house, then turned back. 'Melissa is going to ask what he was doing out there, but I can't tell her.'

'We don't know for sure,' Wheeler said. 'I think that's all we can say. There's no sense in making her defend him by telling her what we think happened.'

She turned toward the house as Ben said, 'Bucky, you and Dave stay here. Long will be around if the Indians start anything. Justin and

161

me will dig the grave.'

Maudie caught up with Cherry before she reached the house. She said, 'Melissa shouldn't see the body because she'll remember it all of her life, but I reckon there's nothing we can do if she insists on it. Just be sure I have time enough to wash his face. That'll make it a little easier on her.'

Cherry nodded and, going into the house, crossed the front room and stepped into the bedroom. Melissa was lying on her side just as she had been when Cherry left her. The shooting had not wakened her. Cherry sat down on the edge of the bed, thinking that the last two nights were the first nights Melissa had slept in a bed since she'd left home. She'd been completely worn out, and Cherry did not doubt for a minute that if she had kept going another day, she would have been a very sick girl.

Cherry did not waken her for a time, but sat on the bed trying to think how she could tell Melissa. The trouble was there were no right words, no way of cushioning news like this. Then she wondered what Melissa would do. Whatever was left of the money Rick had stolen would have to go back to his folks. That would leave Melissa with nothing except the horses and saddles. By rights they should be sold and the money they brought taken back to Boulder, too.

One thing was certain, Cherry told herself.

162

Melissa could not go home. Maudie would keep her, or she could stay here. Cherry knew Ben wouldn't object. She remembered Melissa asking if she and Rick could get work somewhere in this country, and she had thought that if Melissa were alone, she probably could. Well, she was alone now, and in time she would find work.

No use putting off a thankless task. Cherry woke Melissa by shaking her. The girl turned, her eyes coming open, but several seconds passed before she was fully conscious and recognized Cherry. She yawned and stretched, then smiled.

'I'll bet breakfast is ready,' she said, 'and I'm being a lazy bones sleeping my life away while you and Maudie do all the work.'

'No, it's early,' Cherry said. 'I've got something to tell you, something that's bad news. I guess it's the most terrible news I could give you.'

Melissa sat up, frightened. 'It's Rick, ain't it? I thought I heard some shooting, then I decided I'd dreamed it and went back to sleep.'

'No, it was real,' Cherry said, and told her what had happened.

For a long time Melissa sat motionless, stunned, unable even to cry. Finally she said, 'I killed him, Cherry. I guess I knew all the time he couldn't take care of himself in a country like this. I could, so I tried to look out for him, but when Maudie made me stay in the house

163

and had him sleep in the barn, I couldn't take care of him.'

'No, you didn't kill him,' Cherry said. 'You might as well say Maudie killed him by putting him in the barn. Or me because I thought she was right. Or Ben because he didn't watch Rick more closely.' She swallowed, seeing the agony that was in Melissa, then she burst out, 'Melissa honey, don't blame yourself. Rick did it. He shouldn't have gone out there and he knew it.'

'He was very brave,' Melissa said in a low, strained voice. 'He kept saying that if he had a gun, he'd chase the Indians back to the reservation. He must have found a gun and tried to do it, but there was just too many of them.'

Cherry remained silent. She wasn't sure Melissa believed it, but if saying a lie of such proportions helped her accept the reality of Rick's death, then the lie had some value.

For a moment Melissa was silent, her face contorted by her grief, then she blurted, 'But I'm to blame. Don't you see? He shouldn't have gone out there by himself, but he never could make the right decisions. I got him to leave home, and ... and ...'

Then the tears came in a great flood, her sobs so loud that Maudie, coming back from cleaning up Rick's body the best she could, heard the girl before she reached the house. She set the washpan on the table and looked into

164

the bedroom. Cherry had an arm around Melissa, holding her and comforting her, and that was all anyone could do.

CHAPTER SEVENTEEN

Ben selected a place for the grave in the sagebrush near the base of the hill. He said to Miles, 'This is as far as we ought to go. We'd better stay close enough to the buildings so we can get to them if the Indians rush us.'

Miles glanced uneasily at the river. He said, 'Then this is far enough.'

'After the trouble's over,' Ben said, 'I'll build a fence around the grave. Might make Melissa feel better. Keep the cows and horses from tromping over it anyhow.'

They finished digging by noon and started back to the house. Ben said, 'You're pretty good at carving, Justin. You'll find two, three boards in the back stall. Pick out the best one for a headboard. Put Bradley's name and the date on it. Maybe later we can find a stone marker.'

Miles nodded. He was only half listening, for he was staring across the river, frowning. He said, 'Ben, a bunch of them red devils just rode out of the timber. You reckon it's some new ones, or did Nosho's outfit go somewhere and decide to come back?'

Startled, Ben glanced at the line of Indians that had just ridden into view below the timber on the west side of the Yampa. He counted ten of them riding single file down the slope. He didn't recognize any of them. At this distance all Indians looked alike.

Ben's first thought was that Nosho and his young braves had become impatient after the shooting this morning and Ben's recovery of Bradley's body and had ridden away, then for some reason had decided to come back. Ben was startled when he noticed that the warrior leading this group was not riding a pinto. It wasn't Nosho and the chances were very good that this bunch were the reinforcements Ben had hoped would not come.

'Probably the same outfit that shot at me this morning,' Ben said with feigned carelessness.

He didn't want to worry Miles, but he was reasonably sure that now there were twice as many Indians as there had been, enough for Nosho to risk an attack. Ben wasn't sure that he would, but the danger was far greater than it had been. He was still thinking about it when he reached the house and met Dave Wheeler who had just left it.

'Maudie says to tell you it'll be about ten minutes till dinner's ready,' Wheeler said.

'Better go find that board and start carving,' Ben told Miles.

'I've been trying to talk to Melissa,' Wheeler said after Miles left. 'I'm afraid I didn't give her much comfort.' Troubled, he ran a hand across his face, then went on, 'I found out all that Melissa knew about the boy. The part that worries her the most is returning the money Rick stole from his father. I promised I'd do it.'

'You'll have a hard time talking to his folks,' Ben said. 'Unless you're a better liar than I think you are, I don't believe you can do it.'

'There are worse sins than telling that kind of lie,' Wheeler said. 'Right now I want you to come with me and get Rick's money. Hank Long's been in the barn with the body. He says he don't dare show himself outside in the daylight because it'll trigger off a fight.'

'He's probably right,' Ben said. 'You're thinking that Long may have stolen Rick's money, which means we'll have to take it away from him.'

'I've been worried about it ever since the thought occurred to me,' Wheeler admitted. 'I judge that Long is less than an honest man.'

'You judge right,' Ben said, 'but we'll handle him if the money's missing. Did Melissa tell you how much was left?'

'She thought it was about six hundred dollars,' Wheeler said. 'He hadn't spent much except for the horses and saddles.' He fell into step with Ben who had already started toward the barn. 'You know of anyone who would buy the horses and saddles? Melissa wants them sold and the money added to whatever we find on Rick's body.'

'Nobody around here has cash to put out for anything,' Ben said. 'You might get a hundred dollars if you had 'em in Denver, but there just ain't that much money floating around in this country. At least I ain't seen it.'

'I'll take them to Denver,' Wheeler said.

'Be a long trip for you,' Ben said. 'I mean, just to go to Boulder and then turn around and come back.'

Wheeler smiled. 'A very long trip, and with exactly two dollars in my pocket, but I'll make out. The Lord will provide. If he doesn't, I'll go hungry.'

'You are coming back?'

Wheeler threw out a hand toward the river. 'The Lord and the Utes willing, I'll come back as fast as I can. Ben, I've had a feeling the last few hours. Seems to me I was brought here for a purpose, and not the purpose of helping Nathan Meeker which was what I had in mind when I left Greeley.'

'You'll marry me and Cherry before you leave?'

'Any time you say.'

'Good. Now about that feeling of yours. I don't expect anything much to happen this fall, but next spring when the Indians are whipped and the news gets out, we'll have families coming over the range by the dozens, hundreds maybe, and they'll be settling all up and down the river. We'll need a church, and that means we'll need a preacher.'

'I'd like to be that preacher,' Wheeler said.

They went on into the barn and, kneeling beside the body, threw back the canvas. Ben unbuttoned Bradley's shirt and pants. His money belt, stiff with dried blood, was still strapped around his waist.

Long, watching them, swore as he saw Ben take the money from the belt and count it. Ben, glancing obliquely at the trader, told himself that Long had never guessed Rick was carrying anything like this amount or he would have taken it.

Ben drew the canvas back over the body and rose. 'No use letting Melissa see the belt. All that blood would upset her, but she may want to look at the money. There's six hundred and four dollars. I guess his pa will be glad to get it back.'

Maudie called dinner. Long said, 'I'm staying right here inside the barn. I seen another bunch ride in while ago. They ain't giving up on me by a long shot.'

'I'll bring a plate out here for you,' Ben said.

He went into the house, Wheeler walking beside him. When they sat down at the table, Ben saw that Melissa was not in the kitchen.

Apparently Cherry read his mind, for she said, 'I took a plate of food to Melissa, but I don't think she'll eat anything.' She glanced at Wheeler. 'Does anybody know when we're having the funeral? I don't know who has the responsibility of picking the time, but it seems

169

to me that somebody has to.'

'I'm picking it,' Ben said, 'though I don't know whether it's my responsibility or not. I'm making it mine because we need to get the burying over with.'

'Why?' Maudie demanded. 'Looks to me like you're sitting on some news. What is it?'

Ben hesitated, glancing around the table. They might as well know, he decided. There were no cowards here. Even Justin Miles had held up his end better than he'd had any right to expect.

'Another bunch rode in a while ago,' Ben said. 'That doubles Nosho's band. I've got a notion he sent out runners while he was hiding in the brush watching us. A runner caught up with at least one other raiding band and it just got here. We're sitting ducks compared to a settlement like Hayden or Steamboat Springs.'

Irritated, Miles glared at him. 'What the hell! While ago you told me...'

'I know what I told you,' Ben snapped, 'but I've been thinking about it. I ain't sure now, but I've got a hunch it's a new bunch and it's my guess more of 'em will be riding in afore dark. I'm still guessing, but the chances are we won't be bothered till about sundown.'

'The sooner we bury him, the easier it'll be on Melissa,' Maudie said. 'It'll be hell any way you slice it, but I think we'd better get it over with.'

'Mr Wheeler,' Cherry said, 'I'd like to sing at

170

the funeral. I'm not a real good soloist, but I'd like to try. It seems like we ought to have some music.'

'Good,' Wheeler said. 'Music often brings the fluttering of angels' wings. I never like to have a funeral without it.' He hesitated, looking at Cherry briefly, then asked, 'What do you want to sing?'

'In the Sweet By and By,' Cherry answered.

'That would be fitting,' Wheeler said.

Ben, watching him, wondered if he had been afraid Cherry would select a song that was not fitting for a funeral. He didn't know her very well, Ben told himself. Cherry had a sense of what was fitting, a quality he had found lacking in many people. It was, in fact, a rare talent, and one he had not fully appreciated in her until the Indian trouble had started.

As soon as Ben finished eating, he rose. 'I'll harness up. We'll take our guns with us. We'll use your wagon, Justin. Mine has the hay rack on it.'

Fifteen minutes later Ben drove the wagon to the house, Rick Bradley's body wrapped in canvas in the bed behind the seat. Ben waited a minute or so until Wheeler came out of the house with Melissa, Cherry and Maudie following. Ben had been watching the brush along the river, but he had seen nothing alarming. Miles and Bucky were standing beside the wagon, Miles on the left, Bucky on the right.

'We're ready,' Wheeler said.

Ben drove out of the yard, his Winchester beside him. Maudie carried her Sharps, and Miles and Bucky had their rifles. Ben glanced back once and saw that Wheeler was walking with Melissa. The girl was very pale. She stared straight ahead. She stumbled as Ben looked at her and would have fallen if Wheeler had not caught her arm.

When they reached the grave, Ben swung down from the seat, his rifle in his hand. He looked at the river again, but he saw nothing except the grass, the cottonwoods, and the wall of brush along the bank. He was playing a hunch that Nosho would respect the burial just as he had respected Ben's efforts to bring the body in early that morning.

Miles helped Ben lift the body from the wagon and lay it beside the grave. Wheeler stood apart from the others, bareheaded under the clear, fall sky. For a time there was silence except for the breathing of the wind through the timber on the side of the hill to the east and now and then the raucous cry of a jay from somewhere among the quakies.

Wheeler broke the mountain silence with the Twenty-third Psalm, and followed it with the Lord's Prayer. He gave a short account of Rick Bradley's life, then he nodded at Cherry who stepped forward to stop at the edge of the grave. She folded her hands in front of her and, tipping her head back, began to sing in a clear, soprano voice.

Ben stared at the girl, spell-bound. He had never heard her sing before. He had no idea she could, and certainly not like this. For the first time in his short, tough life, he thought he felt the presence of God.

No one moved from the moment Cherry sang, 'There's a land that is fairer than day,' to the end of the last chorus, 'We shall meet on that beautiful shore.' Finished, she stepped back to stand beside Maudie and Melissa.

For a time the only sound was the muffled crying of the women, then Wheeler lifted a hand and began to pray, asking God to receive Rick Bradley's soul and have mercy upon it and to comfort those who had loved him.

Wheeler said, 'Amen.' Turning to Melissa, he took her arm and led her back across the narrow patch of sagebrush to the house, Maudie and Cherry falling in behind them. Ben nodded at Bucky who nodded back and followed the others.

Miles helped Ben fill the grave, both men hurrying. A sense of urgency had tightened Ben's nerves and he was certain that Justin Miles felt it more strongly than he did. Finished, they shoved the headboard into place at the head of the grave, then threw the shovels into the bed of the wagon and climbed up to the seat.

On the way to the barn, Ben thought about how much Miles had changed, once he had made up his mind he had to carry his share of the load. On impulse Ben said, 'It strikes me you turned out to be a hell of a good man, Justin. What was the matter with you before?'

Miles shot a glance at him, then looked away. 'I just never liked to work, Ben. I'd have been all right if I'd never got married, but I wasn't cut out to support a wife and daughter. I reckon the things Cherry has said about me are right. I've always been shiftless, judged by her standards. Yours, too.'

'Maybe it'll be different after this Indian scare's over,' Ben said. 'Maybe you'd like to stay here and live with us.'

Miles's mouth fell open. He looked at Ben as if to see if he were serious, then he shook his head. 'I never expected to hear that out of you. No, it wouldn't do. When this is over, I'll be just as shiftless and lazy as ever. It's the way I like to live and Cherry's nagging won't change me. I can make out by myself if I don't have to look after anybody else, just hunting and fishing and working when I feel like it. No, it just wouldn't do.'

Justin Miles was honest, Ben thought, more honest than might be expected. He was probably right, too. Once the emergency was over, he would fall back into his old way of life, so it was just as well he didn't stay and annoy Cherry. Ben knew she would be annoyed. And Miles was right about Ben having his standards. He couldn't stomach a man who, judged by those standards, was shiftless and lazy.

They unhooked and led the horses into the barn. Ben said to Long, 'Help Justin with the horses.'

The trader stared at him insolently, then apparently decided it was not the right time to defy him, so he turned to one of the horses and began to strip harness from the animal.

'You think you're purty damn smart, Holt,' Long said, 'fetching the body in this morning like you done and having the funeral and getting off scot free. Now I'll tell you something about them damned Utes. The thing they respect is guts, and you running around like you had the world by the tail and not acting scared of 'em has got 'em to thinking you've got guts. Trouble is, they still want me and they'll come after me. When they do, you'll either let 'em have me or you'll all get wiped out.'

Ben turned on his heel and left the barn. Hank Long knew the Utes better than he did, but he still wasn't sure Long was right. He was of the opinion that if the Indians were worked up enough to make an all-out attack, they wouldn't be satisfied with Long's scalp.

Bucky, standing in front of the house, pointed across the river and called, 'Look at 'em, Ben.'

He turned and felt his breath go out of him. Another line of mounted warriors had appeared on the slope below the timber. There were twenty or more of them in this bunch, so again Nosho's band was doubled. Now they would attack, Ben told himself.

'Come on,' he said. 'Let's get into the house.'

He ran through the front door, Bucky at his heels. Justin Miles and Long were in the barn, and that was where they would have to stay, at least until dark.

CHAPTER EIGHTEEN

The instant Bucky was inside the house Ben closed and barred the front door. He turned to a window and watched the new band of Utes ride toward the river. Wheeler stepped out of the bedroom as Maudie and Cherry rushed into the front room from the kitchen, Maudie demanding, 'What's going on?'

'You'd better come and look,' Ben said, motioning for Wheeler to join him. 'Bucky, bar the back door. It'll take 'em a while to get organized, but it might not be very long at that.'

Maudie and Cherry crossed the room to the other window, then Maudie began to swear. Finally she swung around to face Ben. 'Ain't there enough of them devils out there now?' she asked as if the arrival of the new band was a personal affront.

176

'Nosho's been real cautious,' Ben said. 'I ain't sure if it's because it's the way he is or if he figures he don't have enough men to take us. We've got a big edge, or had one, I mean, forted up inside the house, but with all the braves he's got now, they could keep coming and bust the door in.'

'Ben, where's Pa?' Cherry demanded.

'In the barn.'

'They'll kill him,' she cried. 'Long's out there and they know it.'

'We can't go to the barn,' Ben said, 'and I sure hope Justin don't take it into his head to come to the house.'

'Why?' Cherry demanded. 'They haven't shot at us. I can run to the barn and get Pa and fetch him back.'

'No, not till dark,' Ben said. 'You might make it because it'd take a purty fair shot from the river to get one of us who was running between here and the barn, but some of the Utes are good shots. I've seen 'em shoot. With the braves they've got over there now they're not going to be in any mood to sit around and watch.'

'But we can't just sit here and wait for them to kill Pa,' Cherry said.

'We don't know they will,' Ben said. 'Justin and Long have got rifles and plenty of shells. The barn's as tight as the house, and Long will be watching every move they make. If the Indians take a whack at us, we'll turn 'em

177

around in a hurry.'

He wasn't at all sure they could do anything of the sort, but he knew the Utes did not fight the way the Plains tribes did. They were used to defending their mountain hunting grounds and had done so successfully for generations. They fought because they had to, not because it was sport as it was with the Cheyennes and Sioux and other Plains tribes who were taught that death was not a thing to be avoided and that it was better to be killed while in the full vigor of manhood than to linger on into helpless old age.

Ben stood at the window considering this as he tried to measure their chances. There were at least forty Ute braves on the other side of the Yampa. The new band had disappeared behind the willows, probably to talk to Nosho.

The point that seemed most important to Ben was whether Nosho commanded the entire force that was over there. If he did, Ben thought there would not be an attack, but if some other chief who was more daring was giving the orders, then there would be trouble.

Maudie and Cherry had returned to the kitchen. Melissa left the bedroom and joined them. Wheeler, standing beside Ben, said, 'Cherry's right. I'm going to the barn. I'll take your Henry rifle and all the shells you've got. That'll leave you and Bucky and Maudie in the house with guns, and it'll put three of us in the barn. That way I think we can hold both buildings.'

Ben nodded, thinking that Wheeler could probably reach the barn safely, but he doubted that the preacher would be able to return before dark. The Indians would be watching and if he tried to come back while it was light he'd draw a hail of lead.

'All right,' Ben said. 'Go out through the back and run like hell. Take a canteen of water with you. When it's dark, I'll come out.' He motioned to Bucky. 'Let him out through the kitchen door, then shut and bar it and get back to that other window in a hurry. If they start shooting at Dave, which I figure they will, we'll give 'em a little lead so they'll know we're on the job.'

Bucky leaned his Winchester against the wall and followed Wheeler into the kitchen. Ben, watching the willows, saw activity on the other side of the river, smoke from the Indians' cook fires and warriors riding back and forth without making any effort to hide themselves. Now Ben thought he had his answer. Here was a show of bravado that Nosho had not allowed, so he was probably not in command.

Ben heard the mutter of talk from the kitchen and Maudie saying above the others that Wheeler was a fool. She stalked into the front room carrying her Sharps and stood at the opposite window from Ben scowling at the activity on the other bank of the river.

'I can put a slug into one of them devils,

179

Ben,' Maudie announced. 'It's a fur piece, but this here old gun will carry that distance.'

'Sure it will,' Ben said, 'but you wait till Dave makes his break for the barn. If they start shooting, let 'em have it.'

'All right, I'll wait, damn it,' Maudie growled.

She knocked glass from the window with her rifle barrel and stood waiting. Ben sighed. The glass had been costly and hard to get and he hated to lose it, but he had no choice. He smashed the glass out of his window and shoved the barrel of his Winchester through the opening as he heard the back door open and slam shut.

Wheeler took off for the barn on a dead run, keeping low and zig-zagging as he ran. He had covered half the distance before the Utes saw him. There was a crackle of gunfire, most of the bullets falling short. Bucky was back in the front room standing beside Maudie at the other window by the time the first Indian fired. Maudie let go with the Sharps a split second before Ben and Bucky squeezed the triggers of their Winchesters.

One brave, who was in plain view on the other side of the ford, was knocked sprawling off his pony as if he had been suddenly sideswiped by an invisible club. Maudie had scored a hit, Ben thought, for he was reasonably sure that neither his nor Bucky's rifles was accurate at this distance.

Cherry, watching from a bedroom window, called, 'He made it.'

The rifle fire died after the one outburst. Maudie crowed, 'I got him. By hokey, I got him. Did you see, Ben?'

'Yeah, I seen him,' Ben said. 'A purty lucky shot.'

'Lucky?' Maudie howled indignantly. 'That wasn't luck. That was good shooting, you ornery son of a . . .' She bit her lip and glared at Ben. 'All right, you done it again. Someday I'm gonna get smarter'n you and not take the bait you dangle in front of my nose.'

She reloaded the Sharps, leaned it against the wall, and stomped across the room to the kitchen. Ben grinned and winked at Bucky, then turned to the window. His grin faded immediately. For the first time he heard the thump-dum-dum of the war drums, a frightening sound that sent prickles racing up and down his spine.

Bucky whirled to face him, demanding, 'What's that?'

'War drums,' Ben answered. 'They'll be doing some dancing now to work themselves up to making an attack, but it may not come for a long time.'

Maudie and Cherry came into the room, Melissa lingering behind them, her frightened eyes whipping back and forth between Ben and Bucky.

'Drums, ain't it?' Maudie asked.

181

'It's drums, all right,' Ben said.

'Then I guess they mean business,' Maudie said. 'Damn it to hell, I've lived out most of my allotted years, but it'd be a shame if you younguns lost your hair and didn't get a chance to live your life out.'

'We mean business, too,' Cherry said. 'They haven't got us yet.'

Ben was proud of her and surprised at Maudie. He said, 'That's right. What we've got to do now is to watch. Bucky and me will take turns in front. One of you women watch from the back. I think they'll come from the river, but we can't take any chances.'

The hours that followed were the longest Ben had ever known. Cherry made coffee along at the tag end of the afternoon and brought a cup to Ben. The sun dropped to the top of the western ridge, then sank behind it, the light slowly fading. This was the time Ben expected the Utes to attack, but they stayed out of sight on the other side of the Yampa.

Maudie hung blankets over the windows of the kitchen and the front room. Cherry called supper. By the time they finished, the darkness was complete. Ben eased out through the back door with supper for the men in the barn. Wheeler opened the door when he called. He slipped inside, pulling the door shut behind him.

A lighted lantern hung from a peg in the wall. Ben looked from one to the other, surprised that he did not sense fear in any of them.

'I figured they'd hit us 'bout sundown,' Ben said, 'but they didn't make a move. You got any notion why they didn't, Long?'

'Yep, I've got a notion,' Long said. 'Nosho wants me. It was his friend I killed. He don't give a damn 'bout any of the rest of you, but this last band that rode in belongs to a chief they call Sergeant. He don't give a damn about me. He wants everybody who's here. He's a Comanche, but he was raised by a Tabeguache family who lived south of here on the Uncompahgre.

'This here Sergeant is a sneaky bastard. He killed a Tabeguache buck and had to get out, so he rode north to White River and joined Jack's band, but purty soon he had a band of his own. They're renegades and they ain't liked by the rest of the White River Utes, so I'm guessing that Nosho and Sergeant have been jawing 'bout how to do this job and who's gonna run the show.'

'If it was Nosho,' Ben said, 'he'd sneak in like they done the other night.'

Long nodded. 'Yeah, but Sergeant probably figures they've got enough men to ride in and fire the buildings or bust a door in. Now they won't do nothing till morning, but if Sergeant fetched some whisky along, you can count on 'em hitting us 'bout daylight. He'll be riding a big, black horse. You'll know who he is when you see his horse.'

'I don't look for 'em to make a move before morning,' Ben said, 'but you'd better keep one man up to watch.'

'We'll do it,' Wheeler said.

Ben returned to the house. Maudie insisted on taking a turn at standing guard during the night. Ben slept three hours, then spelled Maudie off at midnight. He doubted that any of the women slept, for the drums kept up the hideous thump-dum-dum.

He could see the glow of several fires on the other side of the river and guessed that the Utes were dancing in anticipation of their victory in the morning. Now, watching and listening as slow minutes ticked by, Ben was convinced that the Indians would attack before sunup whether they had any whisky or not.

Ben pulled the blankets down from the windows when the first gray light of dawn began trickling across the valley. Then, realizing the drums were silent, he woke Bucky and Maudie and told them to wash their faces with cold water, that they'd better be in shape to shoot. Cherry woke and, dressing quickly, came out of the bedroom, but Melissa, completely worn out, continued to sleep.

Maudie and Bucky were at the other window when Cherry emerged from the bedroom. Ben said, 'The shells for the Winchesters are on the table, Cherry. Move 'em to the floor so you can stay flat. I'll hand my rifle to you to load when it's empty. I'll use my revolver while you're loading. If we can throw enough lead at 'em, we'll persuade 'em to slope back across the river.'

'Maybe,' Maudie said. 'Don't count on it.'

'Here they come,' Bucky yelled. 'Must be a million of 'em.'

'Hold your fire till you know you can hit something,' Ben said.

The Indians crossed the river at a brisk pace, a warrior on a big black in the lead. That, Ben thought, would be Sergeant. He didn't come directly at the house, but angled away from it until all his men were across the Yampa; then he raised his rifle and screamed a derisive taunt.

Sergeant put his black into a run and circled the house and barn, his men stringing out behind him. Ben, scanning the long line of Ute warriors, did not see Nosho's pinto and wondered if this meant that the Indian was still hiding in the willows.

Maudie let go with her Sharps, knocking a horse down and sending his rider sprawling head over heels, so shaken up he didn't move for a minute or more. A moment later Ben and Bucky began to fire, even though the range was still too long for their Winchesters. The Utes were shooting across their ponies, leaving very little of their bodies showing.

Bullets ripped into the log walls of the house. Now and then a slug snapped through one of the windows to lodge in the opposite wall.

Melissa woke screaming and, opening the bedroom door, stood there with nothing on but Ben's shirt, the screams continuing to come from her open mouth as if she had lost all power to stop them.

'Get down,' Cherry cried. 'Flat on the floor.'

Ben emptied his rifle and handed it to Cherry to reload. He whirled back to the window, his revolver in his hand. Melissa, whimpering now, crawled on her hands and knees to where Cherry lay on the floor.

A bullet splintered the window casing beside Maudie and drove a sliver into her cheek. She cursed the Utes and all of their misbegotten ancestors as she wiped the blood across her face making her look as if she were wearing a red mask. She pulled the trigger of her Sharps, slamming a slug into the side of a horse and knocking him sprawling on top of his rider.

The men in the barn were firing, too. Ben, dropping his empty revolver back into the holster, took the loaded rifle from Cherry. He turned to the window in time to see Sergeant uncoiling the circle by leading the band of Utes back to the ford.

Within a minute or two the shooting stopped. Several dead horses made dark lumps on the grass in the thin dawn light. Two dismounted warriors ran toward the river. Maudie's Sharps boomed again, but this time she missed. Both of the fleeing Indians reached the willows. Another brave, who must have

186

been wounded in a leg, was worming his slow and tortured course through the grass.

'Well, by hokey,' Maudie said as if she couldn't believe what she saw. 'How do you account for that, Ben?'

'I ain't sure,' he said, watching the last of the mounted Indians cross the river. 'For one thing they probably hit a hotter fire than they expected. Maybe this first attack was just to feel us out. If they come again, I look for 'em to try to burn the buildings.'

Melissa began to cry. Cherry pulled her to her feet and, putting an arm around her, took her back into the bedroom. Bucky leaned against the wall, his head down, his shoulders drooped.

'You sure done good,' Maudie said, patting Bucky on the back. 'Maybe we just gave 'em more'n they figured on.' She stood her Sharps against the wall. 'I'm gonna start a fire, Ben. We all need a good, hot breakfast before they come again.'

'Maybe they won't come again,' Ben said.

'Now what the hell are you talking about?' Maudie asked irritably. 'Of course they'll come again. You don't need to...'

'Come here,' Ben said. 'Looks to me like Sergeant got some news we ain't heard. They're pulling out, but it ain't because we whupped 'em.'

Maudie ran to the window. The Indians were riding up the slope beyond the river and

187

disappearing into the timber. 'I'll be a hop toad's uncle. I thought you was bulling us, but they are leaving. Aw, this ain't sense, Ben. We didn't give 'em that hot a reception and that's a fact.'

'No, but I'm guessing they're afraid somebody else will,' Ben said. 'I'm going out to the barn. You get that breakfast started.'

He went out through the front door and sucked in a long, deep breath, thinking that just a few minutes ago he had been afraid he would never walk through his front door again and take another breath of fresh air that was free of the stench of burned gunpowder. It had been close, he thought. Too close.

Wheeler, Miles and Long left the barn and walked toward him, Miles calling, 'I guess we gave 'em hell, didn't we?'

'Yeah, we sure did,' Ben said, thinking again that Justin Miles had been a pleasant surprise. 'Maudie's getting breakfast. I'll stay outside till you get done, then you come out and I'll go in and eat.'

'I guess I'll go into the house and put my feet under a table,' Long said, smirking. 'I won't have to worry about any of them red devils hiding in the brush waiting to put a window in my skull.'

'You start bragging around Maudie and she'll go to looking for that rope again,' Ben said.

Long turned sullen. 'I'm hanging onto my

rifle,' he said, and followed Wheeler and Miles into the house.

Ben turned to look at the windows, the glass gone, but he had no complaint. He was lucky to have his buildings standing. Then he wondered if his luck would hold. Long was here and alive. Maybe this wasn't over.

CHAPTER NINETEEN

Ben had finished breakfast when Wheeler called from the front porch. 'Company coming.' Ben ran outside, all the others except Melissa following. A single rider was coming up the river. Minutes before the man reached the house, Ben was reasonably sure what he would say. The relief column had reached the Yampa.

The man pulled up, dust swirling around him and his horse. He said, 'Colonel Merritt is on his way to Milk Creek. He's got about one hundred and fifty infantrymen in wagons and four companies of cavalry. He figures to reach Milk Creek early Sunday morning. Maybe earlier.'

'Get down and have breakfast,' Ben said. 'This is good news you brought. We don't want you to ride away hungry.'

The man shook his head. 'A lot of folks who are in Middle Park will want to hear the news,

189

too. I'd like a cup of coffee, though, if the pot's on the stove.'

'It's on the stove and it's hot,' Cherry said. 'I'll fetch a cup for you.'

As she disappeared into the house, Ben said, 'I'd say it's a pretty fair guess the raiding parties are getting back on their side of the reservation line.'

The courier nodded. 'You bet they are. It was fun to ride around and burn ranch houses, but they ain't gonna stand and fight a big outfit like Merritt's bringing in. Chances are more soldiers are on the way.'

'There was a big band of Indians on the other side of the river,' Ben said. 'They pulled out while ago. We figured they had some news we didn't.'

Cherry came out of the house with a cup of steaming coffee. The rider reached down and took it as he said, 'Sure they did. They had scouts riding all up and down the river, and chances are they knew the relief column was coming long before any of us did.' He took a sip of the coffee and grinned at Cherry. 'That's good, ma'am. Mighty good.' He took another sip, then asked Ben, 'You have some trouble?'

'A little,' Ben said.

'Lose any men?'

'One.'

'Too bad.' The courier shook his head. 'If you'd all lit out for Middle Park, you'd have been safe.' He finished the coffee and handed the empty cup to Cherry. 'Thank you kindly, ma'am.' He nodded at the men and rode on up the river.

'Well,' Maudie said in exasperation. 'We'd have been safe if we'd lit out for Middle Park, would we? I guess Rick Bradley would have been safe if he'd stayed in the barn where he belonged.'

Justin Miles stared at the courier's back. He said slowly, 'Hard to believe it's over.'

'I ain't sure it is,' Ben said, studying the brush along the river. 'I didn't see Nosho's pinto in the bunch that pulled out. Could be Nosho's still hiding.'

'I thought you said a minute ago that the raiding parties were ...' Bucky began.

'I said it was a fair guess,' Ben said. 'That's all it is. If Nosho's a good enough hater, he's still waiting for Long to show his ugly face.'

Ben scratched the back of his head, not sure what he should do. He saw nothing alarming in the brush, but that didn't prove anything. Except for the attacks and their firing at Ben when he'd gone after Bradley's body Ben had the feeling they might as well have been fighting ghosts.

'Come to think of it,' Bucky said thoughtfully, 'I didn't see that pinto of Nosho's, neither.'

'Did you, Dave?' Ben asked.

'No, but I guess I wasn't looking real close,' Wheeler admitted. 'I couldn't think of anything except that they were leaving and we were still alive.'

Justin Miles had disappeared into the barn. He had harnessed his horses, and now he led them to the wagon and began hooking up. Cherry gripped Ben's arm. She said, 'He's not leaving, is he?'

'Looks like it,' Ben said.

'He can't,' Cherry said. 'Not if some of the Indians are still hiding along the river above here. He'll drive right past them and they'll kill him.'

Ben looked at her. He said, 'Tell me something, Cherry. Did you ever change Justin's mind once he had it made up?'

'Not very often,' she admitted.

'We've got to tell him,' Wheeler said. 'Cherry's right. All of us ought to stick close to your house today.'

'Naw,' Maudie said. 'They're gone. Me'n Bucky will pull out purty quick. Melissa's gonna live with us. I'll go tell her to get ready.'

'How do you know?' Ben demanded. 'You got eyes that can see right through the brush? You didn't have them kind of eyes before.'

Maudie laughed. 'No, I ain't got eyes like that, but the feller that brought us the word rode up the river and nothing happened to him.'

He didn't argue with Maudie, but he told himself that what she said about the courier didn't prove anything. Hank Long was the man Nosho wanted, not the courier. They might want Justin Miles, too.

Miles drove up in the wagon and stepped down, glancing obliquely at Cherry, and then turned to Ben and held out his hand. He said, 'Ben, in the two years I lived across the river from you, we didn't neighbor much and I guess we didn't like each other much. I never thought I'd say it, but I'm saying here and now that you pulled us through. That makes you a hell of a good man.'

Ben shook his hand, surprised and pleased. He thought that the last three days had changed all of them except Hank Long, but Justin Miles had been changed the most of all.

'You fooled me a little, too,' Ben said.

'Don't go, Pa,' Cherry said.

Miles glanced at his daughter, then brought his gaze back to Ben. 'What's the matter with her?'

'We were just talking about it,' Ben said. 'Maudie thinks the Utes are all gone, but I ain't sure. I think there's a chance Nosho and a few of his bucks are still hiding along the river waiting for Long. If they are, they might cut you down as you drive past.'

Miles smiled as he turned back to Cherry. 'It's real good to know that you're concerned about your old pa, but I've got to go now that I got my courage worked up. Maudie here is a tough old bird, but she's pretty smart. I'll take her word that they're all gone.'

Maudie slapped him resoundingly on the back. 'Sure I'm a tough old bird, Justin, and you're no damn good, but I kind o' hate to see you leave here broke. I'll give you twenty dollars for your hay that's in the shock and your wood.'

'Well, I...' Miles began.

'I know I'm the biggest robber on the Yampa,' Maudie said amiably. 'I'm ashamed of myself, knowing your hay and wood is worth more, but who else would buy it?'

'Nobody,' Miles said gloomily. 'You got a deal.'

She handed him two gold eagles, saying, 'Now you're richer'n I am.'

Miles shook hands with Wheeler and Bucky, then stood looking at Cherry, not knowing what to say or do. He sighed and started to turn to the wagon. 'Oh, Pa,' Cherry said, and, running to him, hugged and kissed him. 'You come back and see us someday. You hear?'

He wiped the hairy back of his hand across his eyes and stepped on the hub of the front wheel and then on into the seat. He said, 'I will. I want to see my grandchildren someday,' and drove off.

They watched in silence for a long time, Ben not realizing how tense he was until the wagon was a tiny speck in the distance. He turned to Cherry and took her hand. 'I think he'll be all right now. Maybe Maudie's right, but I've still got a hunch they want Long so bad they'll pass up everybody else in the hopes he'll show up.'

'You know,' Maudie said, 'that old goat of a Justin may be a man yet. He sure done better in this fracas than I ever thought he would. I figure he was born too late. He should have come along when Jim Baker did. Look at him. Got two Indian wives and he's plumb happy.'

Cherry wasn't listening. She stared at the barn as she said, 'Ben, do you think Hank Long is going to stay here?'

'He sure ain't,' Maudie snapped. 'If you think that's what's in his little pin head, I'll go put a bee under his tail.'

'No you won't,' Ben said. 'If there's any bee-putting, I'll do it. I've been thinking about him. I'm as sure as I can be of anything that he's the cause of most of our trouble, but I still can't just sit here and let him ride off without at least telling him what I think.'

'Oh, for God's sake,' Maudie said in disgust. 'Ben, I reckon if you found a rattlesnake in bed with you, you'd make a pet out of him.'

'Ben's right,' Wheeler said. 'I know how he feels. I felt the same way when I brought him here, though I admit I didn't know how much of a scoundrel he was.'

'There he goes now,' Bucky said. 'He's headed for the corral and he's gonna saddle that chestnut of his.'

'You let him go, Ben,' Maudie said darkly. 'You hear me?'

'I won't make him stay,' Ben said, and

195

started toward the corral.

'Ben Holt, what are you going to do?' Maudie bellowed.

'Tell him I think Nosho's waiting to kill him,' Ben said, and kept on toward the corral.

Long was tightening the cinch when Ben reached him. He glanced up, saw who it was, and let his whiskery face grin briefly. 'Come to tell me good-bye, Holt? Or maybe you like my company so good you don't want me to leave.'

'No, I didn't come to tell you good-bye,' Ben said, 'and I sure as hell don't like your company.'

'I'm surprised.' Long spat a brown stream of tobacco juice in Ben's direction, then wiped his mouth with his sleeve. 'Well sir, I watched Miles ride out, thinking that maybe some of them red devils was still hiding along the river, but he didn't have no trouble, so I figure I won't neither.'

Long waggled a dirty forefinger at Ben. 'I said to myself that that bastard of a Miles would have hung me if he could. So would the Kregg woman, only I can't get at her, but I can catch up with Miles and get back at him.'

'I'll get on your tail and chase you till I catch you,' Ben said furiously, 'and when I do, you'll wish the Utes had killed you.'

'No you won't,' Long said. 'You'll never catch up with me. Another thing I want to tell you. I lied about the Indian kid I shot. I killed him dead. That's why Nosho wants me so bad.'

'It would sure be justice if they got you,' Ben said.

Long cackled. 'They won't. I seen 'em ride out of here this morning.'

'I think Nosho's hiding till you come by,' Ben said. 'I don't think that Justin getting away without trouble has got anything to do with you.'

Long cocked his head and chewed for a moment, then he said, 'You're a bad liar, Holt. Did you see Nosho hiding in the brush? Did you smell him? Did he send you a message that he was waiting for me?'

'No,' Ben admitted.

'You're sure easy to see through,' Long said. 'You don't want me to catch up with Miles. Well, it won't work. I'll get him. I've got a good memory on me. When a man wants to hang me for nothing I ever done to him, I figure it's only fair that I get back on him. I will, too.'

Long mounted and, digging his spurs, put the chestnut into a gallop. Ben walked slowly back to where the others waited in front of the house. He had never, he thought, seen a man as completely worthless and vicious as Hank Long. It had not occurred to him to thank Ben for stopping Maudie and Miles from hanging him or for feeding him and his horse. No, the only thought he had was to get even with Justin Miles.

'Well,' Maudie said when Ben came up, 'I see you didn't talk him into staying.'

'I didn't try real hard,' Ben said. 'I've had to deal with some no-good men in my life, but Long's the worst of the lot. He claims he's going to catch up with Justin and settle the score with him.'

'Why?' Cherry demanded. 'Pa never hurt him.'

'He wanted to hang Long,' Ben answered, 'and Long says he's got a good memory. Maybe it's as good as Nosho's.'

Maudie sniffed. 'He didn't have the guts to tackle me.'

'I'm worried about Justin,' Ben said. 'Hard to tell whether Long was just talking big or not, but he's the kind who could do what he said he was going to. Justin wouldn't expect no trouble with him, so it'd be easy for Long to ride up and shoot him.'

'I wouldn't worry none,' Maudie said. 'Long's all wind. I...'

She stopped, staring bug-eyed at five Indians who seemed to explode out of the brush in front of Long, so suddenly and violently did they come. Nosho, riding his pinto, was in the lead.

'Bucky, get inside the house and stay there,' Maudie screamed.

Maudie grabbed Cherry by the hand and half dragged her through the front door. Ben, a step behind them, snatched up his Winchester and Henry from where they leaned against the wall and ran outside. He handed the Henry to

198

Wheeler as Bucky, ignoring Maudie's orders, ran outside with his rifle.

'Watch 'em,' Ben said. 'They're after Long now, but they may be on our necks in a minute.'

Long screamed in terror as he whirled his horse and started back toward Ben's corral on the run, but he didn't have a chance. Nosho's pinto outran the chestnut just as the trader said he had the day of the race. Long did not go more than fifty yards until Nosho was within ten feet of him. He raised his rifle and shot the trader in the back. Long threw up his hands and tumbled out of his saddle, his horse coming on toward the corral he had left a few minutes before.

Maudie ran outside with her Sharps. She dropped to one knee and was lifting the big gun to her shoulder when Ben grabbed the barrel and forced it to the ground. He said harshly, 'Hold up. Let's wait and see what they're going to do.'

The other Utes had reached Nosho by now. They formed a circle and rode slowly around Long, firing at his body as fast as they could pull the triggers of their rifles. There wouldn't be enough left of him to bury, Ben thought.

Suddenly Nosho wheeled his pinto and brought him rearing up on his hind legs. He brandished his rifle above his head and let out a great yell of defiance, then swung his pony and disappeared into the willows, the rest trailing after him. A moment later they came out of the brush on the other side of the Yampa, raced across Justin Miles's meadow, and disappeared into the timber on the slope west of the river.

Cherry ran out of the house as Maudie got to her feet. Maudie stared at her Sharps, and then in a burst of rage threw the rifle on the ground.

'By glory,' she yelled, 'if I'd hit one of 'em, I'd have fetched the whole kit and kaboodle right down on top of us, and all the time they didn't want nothing but Hank Long's hide.' She squared her massive shoulders and glared at Ben. 'I'm glad they got him. You hear?'

Ben didn't say anything. He heard, all right. He couldn't do anything else the way she was yelling at him. He turned to Cherry and slipped an arm around her waist and hugged her.

'It really is over now, isn't it?' Cherry asked.

'Yes, I think it is,' Ben said, 'and we've got another burying job to do. Bucky, you get a shovel and start digging a grave beside Bradley's. Dave, you want to help me fetch Long in?'

'Of course,' Wheeler said.

Ben started toward the barn, then stopped as Cherry laid a hand on his arm. 'Tomorrow?'

'Today,' he said. 'I've got an idea Dave wants to pull out early in the morning with Rick's money. It's a long ride to Boulder.'

'We'd better go get a cake to baking,' Maudie said. 'Looks to me like we've got a wedding supper to fix.'

A funeral and a wedding in the same day! Well, it would not be a funeral like Rick's, Ben thought. There would be no tears shed at Hank Long's burial. Maybe it was wrong to feel the way Maudie did, to actually be glad Long was dead, but on the other hand, Ben was relieved about Justin Miles. If this hadn't happened, Ben would have gone after Long and probably killed him, or been killed by him.

He paused at the corral gate to look at the gold streaks the aspens made on the hills across the river, then he noticed a flock of birds swoop down over the ford to light in a cottonwood farther downstream. A cottontail hopped out of the brush, paused, and disappeared.

Ben smiled as he stepped into the corral. The waiting ... the suspense ... the terror ... all were over. The good days were ahead.